YES, YOU  A 

by

Edweard Deadwitt

and

Murray Ewing

Published by Bookship, 2017.

ISBN 978-0-9934239-4-9

YES, YOU ARE A MONSTER

BOOKSHIP

CONTENTS

INTRODUCTION

"Even a journey of a thousand miles begins with a single step. But if you're a giant, fire-breathing, radioactive lizard-monster, one step might actually be a thousand miles..."

"I can't talk now! Can't you see I'm in my secret lair?"

WELCOME...

Welcome to the first day of the rest of your life.

No, scratch that. Too clichéd. Try again.

Welcome to the beginning of a brief, glorious burst of riotous self-indulgence followed by years of lonely incarceration—

No, scratch that. Too honest. I'm trying to *sell* this baby, aren't I?

Okay...

Welcome to the Introduction.

That's better.

This book will change your life.

A bullet in the head will change your life, too.

This book will change your life in a slightly better way than a bullet in the head.

But only slightly...

It certainly won't change your life as *much* as a bullet in the head. I mean, that's a pretty life-changing event. A bullet in the head can — in fact, most likely *will* — be a life-*ending* event. That's where this book is so much better than a bullet in the head. Reading it won't actually *end* your life.

Or probably won't.

Not immediately, anyway.

Look, I'm not making any guarantees, okay?

What, then, *can* we say about this book?

This book is about you and your inner monster.

You don't have an inner monster?

Yeah, right.

This book is a guidebook to *finding* your inner monster.

You know those old Medieval maps that had "Here Be Monsters" in the blank spaces, where people hadn't explored yet?

This book's like that. Only, the map is of you, and the "Here Be Monsters" covers the whole of it.

Because, let's face it, you're pretty monstrous, aren't you?

Oh, you're not?

Yeah, *right*.

This book is about bringing out your inner monster.

Now, you're probably thinking, "Bringing *out* my *inner* monster?" and how that conjures up an icky image of something wild and alien-looking bursting out of your insides in a splatter of blood and yucky, not-easily-identified red bits, leaving you a twitching mess, a discarded and broken eggshell, while this wild and alien-looking *thing* runs amok in your gloopy remains.

Yeah...

That's *exactly* what I mean.

Now, you're probably wondering, "Why would I want my inner monster to come out?"

But here's the great thing: there isn't a *why*.

There's no reason to it at all.

That thing's going to come out anyway.

You didn't even have to buy this book in the first place!

Ha!

I got you there, didn't I?

Ha!

Oh, you're just reading the free preview chapters?

Damn...

Okay, let's go back to:

This book is going to change your life.

And I'd better not say anything more specific than that.

A word about me

Five years ago, I was a head-case. I don't mean I was a glass jar in which a pickled, severed human head could be kept — though, at the time, it sort of felt like that. No, what I mean is, I was a mess. A mess in all sorts of ways. My wife had divorced me, and I'd been fired from my job. The fact that it felt like my wife had fired me and I'd been divorced from my job probably shows how much of a mess things were. My boss was filing for alimony, my wife was after me for all the paper clips I'd been stealing from her...

I really *was* a mess.

I mean, what was I going to do with all those paper clips?

That's when a friend of mine told me about the miracle of Self Help books. This friend — let's call him Scumsucking Bastard Sam, because Sam was his name, and he was, I later decided, a Scumsucking Bastard — was very fond of Self Help books. He had hundreds of them. He'd read them all. He'd done what each and every one told him to do and it had, he said, turned his life around. When he'd started reading Self Help books, *his* life had been a mess, too. He'd also lost his wife, and his job. Now he still had no wife, and still had no job, but he had a little cart he pushed around the streets selling secondhand Self Help books. I mean, it was something, yeah?

Anyway, he started lending me Self Help books. I read the books. I did what they told me to do. I started each day with my Affirmations. Pretty soon I had a list of Affirmations so long it took me most of the day to say them. They left me exhausted. All those "I *am* this" and "I *am* that", those "I *will* do this" and "I *will* do that". "I *am* in control of my life, I *am*," I'd chant in front of the bathroom mirror, then turn the page to see what to do next.

Some of the books told me therapy might help. I started seeing therapists. I saw strict Freudians and lax Jungians; I saw people who practised CBT, NLP and DIY. And yes, I came away with answers. I came away with so many answers I didn't know what to do.

Finally, one day, I found myself wandering the streets of my home town, utterly broken. My life was in ruins, and no amount of positive thinking, or confessing my innermost feelings to a man with a notepad, a diploma and a Serious Beard, could put it back together. Bereft, destroyed, I wandered till the streets got dark.

And then I thought: I *like* the dark.

No — I *love* it.

In the dark, no one can see you for the shameful no-hoper you are. No one can see your irredeemable, DNA-deep ugliness. No one can see the patches on your elbows or the wax in your ears. Even better, no one can see you as you creep up on them, bare your fangs, and take a bite out of their shoulder.

YES! I shouted. I LOVE THE NIGHT!

"Keep it down, some of us have to work in the morning," said a voice from a nearby house.

"Sorry," I said.

But I *didn't* feel sorry. Not sorry at all. And I *liked* not being sorry. I *loved* it. Because I was—

I was—

Yes—

I was...

A MONSTER!

As soon as I admitted it to myself, everything made sense. All those years wasted on Self Help books, which were written for normal human beings. Of course they couldn't help me. I *wasn't* a normal human being. I was — I am — say it again! — A MONSTER!

Immediately I called my therapist and told him.

Immediately, he called the police.

But that's beside the point. Because now, from my lair in the comfortably padded recesses of the County's deepest, darkest hole, I pen this, my manifesto (I say "pen this", but "crayon this" would be more appropriate, considering the implement I wield between the toes of my right foot, my hands being, alas, strapped to my sides in overlong, holeless sleeves), in the hope that it will help you, too, discover your inner monstrousness — will help you run free, howling and growling, beating your chest and breathing fire, tearing down power lines and snapping up beautiful young things in your massive, hairy claws.

You, too, can be a monster.

I can show you how.

And if, in any way, this book at all earns your gratitude for freeing you from the chains of social restraint, the thumbscrews of peer pressure and the manacles of normality, all I ask in return (aside from the cover price — I have to be kept in crayons!) is you do one thing for me:

Find that Scumsucking Bastard Sam and rip him to pieces, the lowdown — dratted — manipulative — grrr! rarr! — GIVE ME BACK MY CRAYONS!!!

How to use this book

Well, first of all, I'd not recommend eating it.

(But if you're going to eat it, why not try it with some fava beans and a nice chianti?)

((I have no idea what a fava bean is.))

The common practice with books like this is to *read* them.

You should know about this, because you're doing it now.

Other than that, you're really on your own.

This particular book is divided into useful sections, and not-so-useful chapters. You can read it from start to finish, or from finish to start, I don't really care. I mean, if you want to read it so it comes out as nonsense, who am I to stop you?

The generally recommended approach, though, is reading it from start to finish. Usually with little pauses between the sentences. If you read it this way, you'll find that the whole thing makes a kind of warped sense. It starts off with a couple of chapters designed to persuade you that Yes, You ARE A Monster (as it says in the book's title). One of these chapters is my very own Monstrousness Test, a test designed to eke out just how much of a monster you really are. Or it may be nonsense. (Most probably, it's nonsense.)

Following that, there's a section on Finding Your Monstrous Self. In it, you will learn to identify the two major types of monster (Rampaging Monsters and Lurking Monsters), and to work with such essential aspects of being a monster as having (i.e., inventing) an Origin Story, forming an Evil Plan, practising a little trick I call The Reveal, and understanding Your Fatal Weakness. Finishing that section, there's another chapter which I can't remember anything about. Let's leave that as a surprise till we get to it.

Then, there's the section on Your Monstrous Life. This is my favourite section of the book, because it's near the end. It covers such aspects of normal life as Relationships (ick!) and Work (yuck!), and how to deal with these now you are no longer a Normal Human Being, but a Monster. (You'll notice I use a lot of capitals in this book. That's because they're easier to write in crayon.) Then there's another chapter, and... I can't remember much about that one either.

Finally, the book comes to an end. All good things must end. But bad things end too, so the fact that it ends is no guarantee this book is a good thing. In fact, this book — and I cannot emphasise this enough — comes with no guarantees. *Life* comes with no guarantees. Oh, apart from death.

Death...

Mmm, death...

Deathy-death-death...

Oh, sorry, was I writing that? I meant to just think it.

Let's move on swiftly to:

Real-life stories: A Teenage Werewolf

Throughout this book, we'll be looking at the real-life stories of monsters, using their hard-won battles and experiences as a way of understanding your own monstrousness.

Let's start with Joe. Joe is a werewolf. Joe has been a werewolf ever since he could remember. While he was a little boy, his being a werewolf was cute, or at most just a bit annoying. His mother could put up with the occasional ripped-up cushion or him leaving his mark on doorposts. It was (as so often in life) when Joe entered the difficult stage of adolescence that his being a werewolf started becoming a problem.

Adolescence is difficult. Spots, tufts of hair growing in odd places, sudden mood swings, intense thoughts about The Meaning of It All balanced by even more intense feelings of Lust, and Guilt, and Lustful Guilt, and (my favourite) Guiltful Lust. And that's just for normal people. For monsters, it's even worse. You get all that, multiplied by monstrousness. So, even more hair, even larger spots, even wider mood swings, and much more monstrous lusts.

And rages. Oh, the rages.

Joe had rages. He couldn't help having them. He was a werewolf. Every full moon, regular as clockwork, he'd hair up and bug out. He'd howl at the moon, he'd chase cars, he'd dig up bones (usually human ones), he'd make his mark on lampposts and he'd tear the odd family pet into small, bloody pieces.

The neighbours got fed up. Every morning after a full moon, they'd wake to find the tibia of a long-deceased family member badly buried in their otherwise perfectly manicured lawn; they'd find scratch marks on their new car's paintwork; they'd find little Tiddles spread in furry clumps over the driveway.

They got together and talked it over. They went round to Joe's house to have a word with his dad. (This is the mildest form of the torch-wielding mob — see the chapter on Relationships for more on torch-wielding mobs.)

Joe's dad decided to have a talk with Joe. He went up to his bedroom. It was mid-afternoon, but the curtains were closed and Joe was still in bed, having spent the previous night rampaging through the neighbourhood. Joe's dad sat on the edge of his boy's bed. "We have to have a talk," he said. "These wild rampages have to stop. The Wainwrights' little daughter is traumatised by finding nothing but a blood-soaked pair of rabbit ears in the hutch of her beloved Flopsy; the Joneses are fed up taking Great Uncle Samuel's bones back to be reburied at the Cemetery; and they're all beginning to talk about just what really happened to little Tommy Sanders last full moon. So I'm saying it now as your father. These wild rampages have to stop. What have you got to say for yourself, Joe?"

And Joe sat up in bed and looked his daddy straight in the eye. Then he bared his fangs and said, "Grrrrrrrrrrrr."

And Daddy left Joe's bedroom pretty sharpish.

Your first growl

A growl is a monster's best friend. It's our calling card, an announcement of our intentions, and an expression of our innermost monstrousness. It says: "I am going to eat you and all your loved ones" — but so much more succinctly and with such *feeling*. Growl a good growl, and no one's going to doubt that you are a monster who means business.

So, a growl is pretty important, and worth practising.

Let's give it a go, then.

Grr.

Pretty simple, huh?

Grr.

If you want, you can make it longer. Just add r's at the end as required.

Grrrrrrr.

For added efficacy, gnash your fangs and grin on the G.

G-G-Grrrrrrr.

Now *that's* a growl.

Grr. Go on, give it a go. Grrrr.

But they're looking at you worriedly as you read this on the bus, eh?

Get used to it.

Exercise: Your daily growl

One growl is not enough. No, no, no. A growl should be part of your daily routine.

> *Start the day with a growl and end it with a howl, with nothing but monstrousness in between!*

Stand yourself in front of a mirror. (If you're a vampire, forget about the mirror.) Now GROWL. Don't growl — GROWL. GRRRR! Go on. Let's see those fangs, were-wolves! Let's see those stumpy broken teeth, zombies! GROWL!

If you're more the Godzilla type, you could try breathing fire at this point. If you're a Frankenstein's monster type of monster, you might prefer to moan piteously, gripping your head and threatening to destroy your reflection. (Go on, do it. You know you want to. Mirrors are cheap, and what's seven years bad luck? You're a monster, you're already in for a *lifetime* of bad luck.)

The point is, you need to FEEL monstrous. Really feel it. Hook your claws and make swipes at the air. Roll your head like you've just bitten into something and are tearing off a chunk of it. Froth a bit. It can be tremendously liberating. (If necessary, chomp on some toothpaste to get the froth going.) Growl like a lion growls, from deep down in the gut.

Are you frightened?

YOU SHOULD BE!

Your daily growl is an important part of your monstrousness routine. Start today!

BUT I'M NOT A MONSTER

So you've growled your first growl and it made you feel pretty good about yourself, pretty vile, pretty monstrous. And for a while you walked around with a certain swagger, a certain pride, and an evil glow of muted power bubbling about in your belly.

Then it began to fade.

You lost that swagger and that pride, and that bubbling in your belly turned out to be trapped wind. You went back to the mirror and this time, instead of growling, you took a long look at yourself. Do you have fangs? No. Do you have scales? No. Do you have claws? No. Are you undead? You may feel like it most mornings, but the answer is no.

Then it hits you.

"I'm *not* a monster!"

Well, I'm here to tell you you're wrong.

Sure, you may not be a hundred-foot-high fire-breathing mega-lizard, or a giant mutant ape with two heads. Not everyone is an *obvious* monster.

But everyone *is* a monster.

How can I be so sure?

Werewolves among us

Next time you go outside, I want you to take a good look a your fellow human beings.

Pick one. Have a long look at this person (but not so long that they come over and offer you a bite of knuckle sandwich), and ask yourself, "How do I *know* he or she isn't a werewolf?"

I mean, unless you've ventured out at night during a full moon (in which case, I'm wondering why you have any doubts you might be a monster), the chances are you can't tell. Werewolves are ordinary-looking people by day, and monstrous wolves by night. Oh, you say, but what about that thing where their eyebrows are supposed to meet in the middle? Well they *pluck* their eyebrows, dummy. Nobody wants to go around *advertising* the fact they're a werewolf, not unless they want a silver bullet in the gullet.

Now pick another person. Doesn't matter who, anyone. Ask yourself, "How do I know *this* person, if he or she drank the right potion, wouldn't do the Jekyll and Hyde thing and turn into a raging fiend?"

Just picture it. They've got that wicked old bubbling brew in their hands, they take a gulp, and the transformation starts. Suddenly, they're not a sweet old lady with a little hand-basket, heading for the shops, they're a great lumbering loon, gibbering, laughing and running amok.

It could happen to anyone.

"Yeah," you say, "but I haven't got a potion, have I? And I've lived through a fair few full moons without turning into a wolf, so you're not telling me I'm a werewolf, are you?"

No. What I'm trying to point out is that certain types of monsters are only fully monstrous in certain situations. All the rest of the time, they've got their monstrousness bubbling away inside of them. Those werewolves, what do you think they're doing when they go on their full-moon rampages? They're letting out all the monstrousness and evil they've been bottling up. And that little old lady with the potion? Think the potion is doing all the work? No! The potion just adds that necessary kick. It's just the excuse. The monstrousness, the urge to rampage, the need to gibber and laugh and run amok, were all there, under the surface, waiting to be let out.

It only needed the right circumstances.

Okay, so in these cases, "the right circumstances" were turning into a wolf during a full moon, and taking a turn-me-into-a-monster potion. Pretty rare circumstances, yes?

So let's consider for a moment:

The Awful Accident

You're in a lab. Picture yourself in a white coat and specs, perhaps with a little lapel badge that says, "Professor X" on it. You've got a beaker of bubbling red stuff in one hand, and an evilly seething test-tube of green stuff in the other. Why you have these two substances in your hands, I've no idea, because you know they're highly reactive and shouldn't be mixed.

Just then, someone calls your name from across the lab, and when you turn to look, they throw a wet cloth at you. It slaps you in the face and it sticks there. Some joke, huh? These scientists!

Of course, your first impulse is to take the cloth off. It's a natural reaction. Totally forgetting you've got a beaker of bubbling red stuff in your hand, you lift it towards your face, with the result that you throw it all over you. Bubbling red stuff clings there, stinging, smoking, burning. You feel a terrible pain. But the cloth is still there. Chances are, if you take the cloth off quickly, most of the red stuff will come off with it. So you lift your other hand, totally forgetting it's holding a test-tube of seething green stuff — and the result is, you throw that in your face, too. And the moment the seething green stuff hits the bubbling red stuff, they go into their dreaded chemical reaction.

Right in your face.

And when the pain is over, when the awful seething, bubbling agony has abated, you pull what remains of the cloth off...

And you're a monster!

Your face is transformed into a hideous travesty of all it once was — of all that made you human. Somehow, that mixture of bubbling red and seething green has left you with all sorts of scars and lumps and tufts of hair. You look, in short, like someone's thrown a lump of putty into your face, then mashed it up with a knife and fork.

Your rage is immense. You immediately grab the nearest jars and bottles and hurl them at your not-laughing-now colleagues. You ransack the laboratory. Then you jump out the nearest window and run howling into the distance, vowing revenge against humankind.

See what happened there?

An awful accident turned you into a monster.

Now imagine exactly the same thing happening, only the bubbling beaker of red stuff is a fizzy cherry drink, and the seething green is lime juice. Exactly the same thing happens, only there's no hideous transformation. You just have a lot of sticky goo on your face that will wash off.

But you don't realise it. You think you're holding two jars of dangerously reactive fluids. For a moment, as you throw them into your face, you think you've hideously scarred yourself for life. So you throw the bottles and jars, you rampage, you jump out the window, you vow revenge...

Then you realise your mistake.

And what do you do then?

Obviously, you decide that the accident, awful or not, unleashed your inner monstrousness — inner monstrousness that was there all along, just waiting to be unleashed. Awful accident or not, it was *there*, all this time.

Inner Monstrousness

It might be bubbling red and seething green liquids, it might be a full moon, it might be a vile potion that makes you a monster.

Then again, it might not.

But do you want to go through your whole life waiting for that rare special circumstance to bring out your inner monster? Do you want it to seethe and rage, deep down inside, until that perhaps-never-to-be-seen day?

Do you?

Of course you don't.

Let it loose now!

Don't wait another second.

The inner monster is *there*. It's been there since day one. It wants out. It wants to rage and rampage. It wants to vow revenge, then *do* revenge. It wants to scream and howl and laugh and throw things.

Can't you feel it, growling away inside, slavering?

Can't you?

Time to turn it loose.

Exercise: The *Fake* Awful Accident

Genuine awful accidents are, let's face it, awful. Nobody would wish them anyone. So what we're going to do is have a fake awful accident, and pretend it was a genuine one. Just, you know, to see how it goes.

So, get a cup — make sure it's a clean one — or better yet a beaker, if you're the sort of person to have a beaker in the house. Fill it with water. Make it cold water if you can, just to add a bit of genuine shock value to the whole thing, but if you're a total wuss, you can make it lukewarm.

If possible, don a white lab coat.

Hold the beaker or cup (we'll call it a beaker from now on, because we're in character) in both hands. Hold it like it's dangerous. Look at that lukewarm water and *see* it bubbling, frothing. Imagine the whole thing a weird colour, like purple or green, or perhaps both, swirling around. Give it some horrible name, like Potion X or Monodioglutosulphurichorriblate, and imagine a skull and cross bones symbol on the side of the beaker.

Now *throw it in your face*!

Feel the agony!

Drop the beaker (or, if it's likely to break, place it carefully on a nearby level surface), then fall on the ground and writhe! Cry out! Moan! (Scream, if you want, but try not to scare the neighbours.) Grip your face in horror and *feel* the change. Feel the flesh sloughing away, soft and malleable as putty. Feel the burning. Feel the horror as all you once were, all that made you human, slips from your face. (You did remember to remove your contact lenses, I hope?) Feel the death of all your normal, human, hopes and dreams.

Now, how does that feel?

Just a tiny bit monstrous?

You might want, at this moment, to hold a claw-shaped hand up to the sky and vow revenge or something. Just go with what seems right.

Then dry your face off, clean the beaker and put it back in the cupboard, and have a nice sit down. Perhaps a cup of tea.

The Demon of Doubt

The Demon of Doubt will always be there, whispering in your ear that you are *not* a monster. It can always find reasons. You don't have fangs, you're not nearly as hideous as you'd like to think, your mother actually loved you... But look, if you can hear the Demon of Doubt whispering in your ear, you are at least partially insane. And if you're at least partially insane, you're at least partially a monster. And if you're at least partially a monster, you're a whole monster, because who ever heard of a half-monster?

In short, the worse you feel about yourself, the more you are a monster.

Also, the better you feel about yourself, the more you are a monster.

The only way you're not a monster is if you sit around thinking you're normal. (And that, I think, is the most monstrous of all!)

So, yes, you ARE a monster.

And if you have any doubts, the next chapter is sure to remove them.

It's all about my patent-pending, thoroughly certified (insane) Monstrousness Test.

THE MONSTROUSNESS TEST

The Monstrousness Test was developed after literally years and years of thinking about other things, getting on with my daily life, twiddling my thumbs in odd moments, and generally making no effort whatsoever towards developing a Monstrousness Test. In the end, it has been carefully scribbled out with my favourite colour of crayon while bored (and partially insane) on a long Saturday afternoon.

Nevertheless, I think it's pretty accurate.

Let's get things started...

...with a warm-up exercise to the Monstrousness Test I like to call the Ugliness Test.

To do this, you will need a mirror, and the ability to see yourself in a mirror. (The vampires among you might commission a portrait, but the chances are you'll drain the blood out of your chosen painter before the end of it. Better to skip this section and save yourself the expense.)

Stand in front of the mirror.

Close your eyes.

Now, we're going to spend a moment thinking of something nice. A field of daisies. A sun-soaked summer playground with kids running around, swinging on the swings, climbing the climbing frame, eating ice-creams. A litter of kittens rolling and tumbling over their sleepy-eyed mother.

Ditto, with puppies.

Now open your eyes...

God, you're ugly, aren't you?

I mean, not just standard ugly, but *offensively* ugly.

You could really do some damage with a face like that.

Give yourself thirty points. And five more if you were, deep down, at least slightly satisfied or relieved to find out how ugly you are.

The quick-fire question round

Indicate, with a tick (or a facial tic), which of the following you agree with:

- Every day, in every way, I'm getting... hairier.
- ...and wartier.
- I have, at least once in my life, entered into a staring match with a cute animal.
- ...and won.
- Ditto, with a baby.
- ...and won.
- When I see people smiling for no reason, I want to trip them up just to bring them back to reality.
- When I see a little kid crying because he or she has just dropped his or her ice-cream, I have to hold back a laugh.
- ...in fact, I don't even bother to hold it back.
- I don't always cut my toenails as short as I should.
- I sometimes file my fingernails into points.
- I daydream about being a two hundred foot high killer robot.
- I AM a two hundred foot high killer robot.
- When I'm alone I often grin evilly.
- I talk to myself. In growls.
- I'm jealous of the attention monsters get in horror

movies. All those people wanting to kill them!

- I sometimes wish at least one of my parents had been from space.
- I often check my forehead to see if I'm developing horns.
- I often run my tongue over my canine teeth to see if they're getting longer.
- I check my palms for hair at least once a week.
- I have often felt the desire to wear a cloak. Preferably a black one, red-lined.
- I *have* worn a cloak. A black one, red-lined. I swept it about me dramatically.
- I wish I lived in a castle.
- ...or a tomb.
- I sometimes envy the dead. And not just for tax reasons.
- I sometimes envy the living.
- I often find myself saying, "When I rule the world..."
- ...even in mixed company.
- I have a list of at least three things I'll do when I *do* actually rule the world.
- ...and they're all despicable.
- I like to move things around in shops without buying them.
- I have signed at least one petition with a made-up name.
- At least once in my life, when asked for directions to a place I know how to get to, I have lied.
- At least once in my life, when asked for the correct time, I have lied.
- When I bite into an apple, I sometimes like to imagine it screaming.
- I like to drink tomato juice. He he.
- I don't want world peace, I want a PIECE OF THE WORLD!

Award yourself one point for each statement you agree with. Three if you found yourself nodding rapidly or at any point punched the air and said, "Ohhh, yes!"

The situations round

Imagine yourself in each of the following situations, and choose the option that best describes your deepest, darkest, and most gleeful impulse.

You are in a busy shop, at the back of a five-person queue. The little old lady at the front is having difficulty counting out the correct change. She keeps saying, "Sorry dear," to the person at the till, and they keep saying, "That's okay. Take your time."

    Do you:

- *Remain in the queue waiting patiently, because we're all going to be old and useless one day? (0 points)*
- *Grumble to yourself about how they ought to open another till? (0 points)*
- *Leave the queue, put your items back, and exit the shop in a loud huff? (0 points)*
- *Start laughing, first quietly, then loudly, then maniacally, until you are foaming at the mouth? Punctuate this with looking at the thing you're queueing to buy and saying in a loud voice, "I want you, oh how I want you! Soon you will be mine! And then the world will know... Yes, the world... And they — shall — suffer..." (5 points)*

Now try this one:

You are at a job interview. The interviewer plainly doesn't like you, and you don't like him, but you need a job, and you know you are qualified for this one. You see him making little notes on your CV, which you have the sneaking suspicion may be doodles.

Do you:

- *Ignore this, and keep answering the interviewer's questions, in the hope you'll win him over? (0 points)*
- *Ask if he's doodling on your CV, and if that means you've got the job? (0 points)*
- *Say that, if he is the sort of person doing interviews for this firm, then it is not the sort of firm you'd like to be working for, in the hope this will wake him up and make him pay attention? (0 points)*
- *Ignore his latest question and launch into a rambling story about how, on your last vacation, you took to casually leaving bits of dead animal on random people's doorsteps, and how this opened up a whole new area of meaning in your otherwise dull, dreary and painful existence? (5 points)*

And now this one:

You are on a first date. The person you're with is getting a little tipsy, and confesses to an occasional kinky impulse. They are obviously testing the water, seeing how far you are willing to go.

Do you:

- *Tell them you were raised to a strict moral code, then ask to be excused so you can wash you hands, ears, and mouth? (0 points)*
- *Confess your own favourite fantasy, pathetic though it is? (0 points)*
- *Suggest we bring the waiter over for his opinion? (0 points)*

- *Ask how they would feel about being surgically transformed into the first of a new race of mindless superslaves willing to do your evil bidding? And then pretend to have forgotten your wallet or purse, so they have to pay for the meal? (5 points)*

The inkblot test

Stare for a full minute (60 seconds) at this inkblot.

Looks pretty icky, doesn't it?

Claim ten points if you imagined the inkblot in red.

Your score

Tot up your score. Or add it up, if you don't know what "tot" means. If you can't add, just think of a number.

How well did you do?

0–30 points: Are you even alive? I mean, come on.

31–70 points: Did someone *lend* you this book?

71–100 points: That's more like it. This is the "room for improvement" scoring band. I'd say you're pretty used to getting odd looks in public, and perhaps the occasional disgusted grimace, and now you know why — you're a monster. Welcome to the club.

101–132 points: I don't need to tell you you're a monster, because most likely (a) you know it and (b) what few friends you have left have repeatedly told you it, too. So now it's confirmed. You don't get a certificate or anything, though.

133 points & up: You are clearly lying, because you can't get a score this high. But lying and cheating is what monsters do, so a double A pass for sheer chutzpah!

Judging your score

Disappointed by your results in the Monstrousness Test? Frustrated? Annoyed?

I don't really care.

I mean, what did you expect? To be told you were one of the most monstrous of monsters? Because chances are, you're not. Let's face it, if you were Count Dracula, would you be having to read a book about being a monster? No, you'd be out there, doing monstrous things. (Or, like me, suffering the consequences.)

But the truth is, the total score you achieved on the Monstrousness Test is not your *real* score. That score was just to get you to do something while you did the test.

No, your *real* score to the Monstrousness Test can be found by answering the following questions:

1. Did you do the Monstrousness Test?
2. Did you do the Monstrousness Test but not write down your score because you couldn't be bothered, then chose the scoring band you most wanted to belong to?
3. Are you currently reading a book about being a monster?

If you answered "yes" to at least one of *these* questions, award yourself 100 points.

If you scored 100 points or more, then yes, you *are* a monster.

Who cares just *how* monstrous you are? Some days you might be very monstrous, other days you might be only a little bit monstrous. You might even have the occasional off-day when you are (ugh!) nice to people. But basically you are still a monster. Let me put it this way: some days I like to dribble from the corner of my mouth and sing naughty alternative lyrics to nursery rhymes; other days I like to fling myself against the padded walls of my current abode and rave about how nobody understands me. Either way, I am still insane.

So, yes, you *are* a monster.

Why quibble over the details, when you could be out there doing monstrous things?

Time to find your Monstrous Self.

FINDING YOUR MONSTROUS SELF

"To err is human. To grrr is so much more satisfying."

"Well, its weakness isn't silver bullets, and it isn't crosses. Next, we try the sink plunger…"

RAMPAGING MONSTERS AND LURKING MONSTERS

There are many types of monster, but one of the key distinctions is between those who Rampage and those who Lurk. Deciding which camp you fall into is one of the major milestones on your road to monsterdom, so let's dive right in and look at these two monster-types.

The Rampaging Monster

What do you feel, right now?

(Apart from a deep satisfaction at having bought this book?)

Somewhere, down there in your monstrous belly, there's a burning, a rumbling, a monstrous growl fighting to be unleashed in one deafening, window-shattering ROAR!

Now, it's not just indigestion, is it?

It's something deeper than that.

It's *rage*.

All monsters feel rage, but it's the Rampaging Monsters who let it loose in the most spectacular fashion.

Rampaging Monsters don't plan. They don't think. They don't try to talk it through. They simply rage. And there's a direct connection, in the Rampaging Monster, between feeling rage and acting on it.

As soon as the mood takes them (and that usually means as soon they're woken from their million-year, frozen-in-ice slumber by a nearby case of atomic weapons testing), Rampaging Monsters want to destroy things. And, wanting to destroy things, they immediately set about doing just that. They destroy things.

They pull down power-lines. They trample on cars. They rip elevated trains from their tracks. They bash into tall buildings, and it's the buildings that come off worse. They glare at pedestrians. They roar and see them run. They pick up one or two and chomp on them. They throw the others away, casually, like empty sweet wrappers.

There are no rules when a Rampaging Monster is on the Rampage. Everything's fair game.

Little old lady crossing the street? Little *flat* lady, more like.

Baby in a pram? Cinders on wheels.

Busload of school kids? A metal box of tasty snacks.

Nearby national monument? Well, you might want to take a moment to pose in front of it, emphasising the juxtaposition of all that your home nation holds sacred, all its ideals and values — and you, in all your insane rampaging monstrousness. Then you SMASH it! Smash it and ROAR!

The Lurking Monster

Somewhere deep beneath the ground is a cavern. A dark cavern. Leading from that cavern are countless passages, ending in a host of hidden doors that enable you, the Lurking Monster, secret access to lots of interesting places. Using these countless passages and hidden doors, you slip out into the night, do your dastardly deeds, then slip back, disappearing like a ghost (unless you *are* a ghost, in which case you disappear like something else — like smoke, perhaps, or a bad smell), leaving only fear in your wake, until you choose to strike again.

Your night's work done, you return to your cavern.

What do you do there?

First, you indulge in a little self-congratulation. You rub your hands, remind yourself of what you've just done — who you kidnapped, what vital part of society's machinery you sabotaged, how you rearranged all the shop signs to spell out rude words — then you let out a maniacal laugh.

But then, mid-laugh, you remember: you're an outcast, a pariah, hated and feared by Those Who Live Above. Your joy in the night's victory palls, you sink to the murky depths of despair, and there's only one thing for it: you immediately start plotting your next dastardly deed.

What shall you do, what shall you do? More kidnappings? More sabotage? More rude words?

Considering all the many wonderful options to choose from, you start cackling that maniacal laugh again. So good does it feel, in fact, that you cross your secret cavern lair to the enormous pipe organ you stole, pipe by pipe and key by key, from a nearby run-down cinema, and installed here, in your cavern, with loving care. And you play on it — play on it, and laugh maniacally!

As you can tell, the Lurking Monster is quite different from the Rampaging Monster. Where a Rampaging Monster is likely to spend no time at all going from the Urge to Rampage to the actual Rampage itself, the Lurking Monster, once he or she (or it, let's not be prejudicial) feels the need for a bit of Societal Revenge, will spend a good deal of time dwelling on it, brooding on it, lurking in his or her (or its) secret lair, plotting, planning, laughing maniac-ally, cursing the world that has ignored/reviled/mocked/tickled them, and occasionally spending time on their favoured Mad Musical Instrument. (Choose your Mad Music-al Instrument wisely. A triangle or kazoo can give the wrong impression.)

When the Rampaging Monster is angry, everyone knows it. The Lurking Monster, often just as angry, keeps it all locked inside far longer than is healthy, boiling up a deliciously poisonous brew of revenge, resentment, clever plotting and utter insanity, before unleashing it on the world. Often, the unleashing will be done at a remove — you'll have built a killer robot to do your work for you, or will have carefully arranged some complex machinery or devious device to make that terrible thing happen so that you can watch, rub your hands with Monstrous Glee (see the end of this chapter for more on Monstrous Glee), then retire once more to your lair, to brood on what you have done, feel the hollow victory of it all, and sink back into despondent gloom at your status as an outcast and pariah. Then to come up with a whole new Evil Plan, in the hope that this time, yes this time, it will relieve, in some small way, the horror that is your daily existence.

So, which are you?

It may seem a difficult question. At this stage of your monstrous life, you don't really want to put your (clawed, hairy, warty) foot down in any one camp.

But really, it's simple. There are two truths I want to share with you. (Actually, there are many more, but some of them will land me in jail.)

Here they are:

All monsters are rampaging monsters.

And:

All monsters are lurking monsters.

How so?

All monsters are Rampaging Monsters

Or, they'd like to be.

The merest glance at the above section where we set out what it is a Rampaging Monster does (a brief recap: a Rampaging Monster goes on the Rampage), and you'll notice one thing. Rampaging Monsters are usually large. Giant, in fact. Often, they're not remotely human. They're prehistoric creatures woken from their ice-bound sleep; they're off-worldly things like Bob the Alien Blob, landed mistakenly on Earth, but while they're here they'll stay for a snack; they're that Giant Ape who's been whiling away a geological era or two on some island in the Non-Specific Pacific, lured to the city by the promise of a tiny blonde in silk.

Given the chance, all monsters would go on the rampage. We're all driven by the need for revenge, or simply the need to let loose a little steam. But the truth is, if most of us were to go up to your average high-rise sky-scraper and punch it, we wouldn't leave much of a mark. And if most of us were to go up to the nearest car — pas-sengers in or not — and try to throw it, we'd just put our back out.

Being a Rampaging Monster is all about opportunity. Chances are, when you were a kid, you, too, built a mini-ature city of toy bricks, peopled it with toy figures, then trashed the whole thing in an orgy of self-righteous rage. And felt better about it.

But as we get bigger, in a strange sense, we get smaller. The toy city just doesn't *do it* for us any more, and the only alternative — a real city — is too big for us to take out our rage in such spectacular fashion.

But I'm not saying you can't go on the rampage unless you're a one hundred-foot-high Mega Lizard. You just have to choose your opportunities. Maybe, one day, you'll find yourself in a miniature village, one of those tourist attractions where everything's built one-to-ten scale, with tiny model people waving at you from tiny model windows. Yeah, go on the rampage there. Leave the real cities to the Mega Lizards, Giant Apes, and Blob-like Alien Entities.

All monsters are Lurking Monsters

Okay, maybe not *all* monsters. I doubt those Mega Lizards, Giant Apes, and Blob-like Alien Entities are ever going to do much lurking. With them, though, it's a matter of scale. (Not scales. Scale.)

And, frankly, intelligence.

There's not much said about Monstrous Intelligence. That's mostly because there's not much *to* say, but here's what *does* need to be said:

When you're a monster, you have to be a monster with *all* of yourself. All of your qualities (or lack of them).

Monsters get rages, yes, and go on rampages (or their nearest equivalent), yes. But monsters have quieter moments, too. Quieter moments when, the rampaging (or its nearest equivalent) done, they sit back and dwell, in a relaxed way, on more refined ways of wreaking havoc and achieving revenge. On long-term plans.

I won't go into Long Term plans here (for more on them, see the chapter "Your Evil Plan"), but this is just one of the many things your average monster will want to do in the down-time between orgies of carnage and rage.

Basically, all monsters are Lurking Monsters when they're not on the rampage. They lurk, simply *being* monstrous. They hide in shadows and watch, with delirious envy, all the Normal People going about their Normal Lives, filled with such contentment and happiness. (Ugh! Let me spit!)

And there are other times, which we could call Monstrous-Me Times, when you just need to be on your own. In your Dark and Shadowy Lair. Surrounded by your own Monstrous Appurtenances — the torture devices, the mementoes of victims past, the crackling electrical apparatus, your favourite coffin — where you can dwell on those subjects closest to your heart (or the hole that passes for it): your need for revenge, your resentment of Normal People, your much-polished Evil Plan, the delicious thrill of your latest victory, the delicious rage at your latest defeat.

A lair is a place to sit and dwell. Brood. Stew. Rage impotently. Shake your fist against the Creator (or lack of one). Gibber. Perhaps write your memoirs.

Every monster needs a lair. Perhaps the only real division between the Rampagers and the Lurkers is how much time they spend there. The real Lurking Monster spends most of his or her time in his or her lair, venturing forth only at night, and when his or her plan is polished to perfection and ready to be put into action.

The thing uniting both Rampaging Monsters and Lurking Monsters — apart from, obviously, the fact that they are monsters — is what they do in the grip of their most characteristic activities. Deep in their lair, or in the midst of a good Rampage, both the Rampaging Monster and the Lurking Monster are united by an excess of Monstrousness, a self-immolating orgy of despicable emotion known as Monstrous Glee.

So, what is Monstrous Glee and how do you get it?

Exercise: Monstrous Glee

Whether you're a Rampager or a Lurker, every monster has to express Monstrous Glee.

What, then, is Monstrous Glee?

(I'll tell you now, it has *nothing* to do with singing.)

Monstrous Glee comes when you express your utter joy

at being both alive (or, in the case of zombies and vampires, un-alive) and monstrous.

Now, it's not good enough to express Monstrous Glee by smiling. Remember, you're a *monster*. Monsters don't do anything by halves. They don't even do anything by ones. Everything is *way* over the top.

Monstrous Glee is *maniacal* laughter. Monstrous Glee is *uncontrollable cackling*. Monstrous Glee is a verbal orgy of delight in explaining how you're going to destroy the world with your new Infernal Device, and how it will be the perfect summation of both your life's work and your burning need for revenge.

You need to get *drunk* on Monstrous Glee.

You need to stagger around and roll your eyes, you need to clutch the air with your claws, you need to gibber, howl, and froth at the mouth.

Most of all, you need to practise.

Practise Monstrous Glee?

Yes, practise Monstrous Glee.

Because Monstrous Glee needn't be reserved only for those moments where you've got your victim in your clutches. It needn't be just for the big victories. Monstrous Glee is all about the sheer joy of being a monster no matter what's going on. You should be able to wake up at the start of the day (or night, for you nocturnals) full of Monstrous Glee, and you should be able to go to bed at the end (or, ditto, the beginning) just as full of it, if not fuller. Monstrous Glee should be the blood in your veins, thrilling its way round your monstrous body (perhaps leaking out at the ragged bits, you zombies), making every moment of every day utterly, gleefully Monstrous.

The great thing about Monstrous Glee is it doesn't have to be reserved for the good moments in your monstrous life — the victories, the feeling you get when your Evil Plan (see the chapter on Your Evil Plan) comes that little bit closer to fruition. Monstrous Glee can also be expressed in situations of stress, too. Why? Because Monstrous Glee is that wonderful dance you dance on the edge of Utter Insanity. Just when the torch-wielding mob corners you and it looks like the end — why not give them a burst of Monstrous Glee? It'll put them off their guard, and besides, you're a monster, you may as well enjoy the bad moments, too. Show enough Monstrous Glee and they might lock you up instead of driving you off the edge of the nearest cliff. If nothing else, it will give them a lingering feeling of doubt that, as you plummet to your inevitable doom hundreds of feet below, you still got more out of your wretched life than they ever got from theirs. (Being a monster is as much about the little victories as the big.)

So, how do you develop Monstrous Glee?

You need to find an appropriate form of expression. Remember, this is *your* Monstrous Glee. You've got to *own* it. You might want to roar and shake your head, bellowing into the night. You might want to clasp an imaginary globe in one fist and crush it while screaming, "At last! At last! My revenge at last!" You might want to howl at the moon. You might just want to laugh. (But make it a nasty laugh. Make it a real cackle-happy, drool-at-the-mouth laugh.)

Be uninhibited. What are you, a monster or a mouse?

(Sorry if you're a were-mouse. But, seriously, a were-mouse?)

Spend at least five minutes a day, every day for a week, practising your Monstrous Glee. After that, surprise yourself every so often with thoughts of just how GREAT it is being a monster, and let loose a little Glee. After a while, this should become second nature. After a bit longer it should become uncontrollable, and you should find yourself jittering with fits of manic laughter at the most inappropriate times. You should find yourself grinning insanely, perhaps frothing at the mouth or at least drooling, at dinner parties, in bus queues, at job interviews — anywhere it's totally inappropriate.

This is when you know you've really hit your stride.

Your life should be one raging moment of Monstrous Glee from start to end.

Begin today!

ORIGIN STORIES

Every monster has an origin story. They were dropped in a vat of seething monster-goo when they were a baby, they were exposed to highly-mutating Zigma radiation when they were a tot, their mother was frightened by a politician while pregnant, and so on.

Humans have origin stories too. They lack self-confidence because their mother didn't love them, they can't sustain a mature relationship because they come from a broken home, they're lonely perfectionists because their lonely perfectionist parents expected too much of them.

But, let's face it, monster origin stories are so much more *interesting*.

I mean, no one wants to stand there at a party being regaled about how your pet kitten was run over when you were ten and, ever since, you've been unable to trust anyone who owns a four-wheel drive. But think of the reaction if you said: "I came to this planet in search of fresh DNA after my home-world was irreparably damaged in the Neutron Wars."

They'll crowd round to listen!

Most likely, they'll block the exits and try to keep you distracted till the men in white coats arrive, too.

But hey, you'll have had your moment!

They'll *remember* you.

And maybe, just maybe, they'll be *afraid* of you.

Origin stories aren't just for parties

But, as it says in the title to this section, origin stories aren't just for parties.

You don't even have to tell your origin story to anyone. As long as *you* know it, then you can, at any time, remind yourself just why it is you've spent so many hours trying to develop a formula for turning human flesh into green slime.

Your origin story is your *justification* for being monstrous.

Better, it's your *excuse*.

It wasn't your fault! It was Government Scientists. It was Cruel Fate. It was Diabolical Destiny.

Better still (the betters get better and better), by having your origin story not involve anyone who can contradict it (i.e., your mother), you don't have to worry about the entire justification for your life's monstrous misery being undermined. A normal person might say, "I'm the way I am because my mother didn't love me," at which point their mother might butt in and say, "Hey, you weren't exactly a loveable child. You used to break wind constantly. It made you difficult to be around." But, armed with an origin story, you never have to worry about that. All you have to do is stare balefully into the distance and mutter, "It was the Quark Ray, the Quark Ray, the awful, burning Quark Ray..."

And who can argue with that?

(Who'd *want* to?)

Exercise: Your old Origin Story

Write down the story of why you are as you are. I mean why you *really* are as you are. All those psychoanalytical things like your big sister used to dress you up in funny clothes, your father used to pull you around by the ears, you were kept locked in the attic during school holidays.

Write it all down (preferably on one small sheet of paper — let's not get into the Misery Memoirs business, here), then do your monstrous worse on it.

Rip it up! Tear it with your teeth! Throw the shreds in the air and slash at them with your claws. Laugh gleefully! Laugh insanely! Dribble, froth, wet yourself, whatever.

All that's over.

It's time for your new origin story.

True shmoo

True?

What, are you kidding?

True is for wimps. True is for normals. True is for boy scouts.

We're MONSTERS.

We're not after *true*, we're after something with heft, with horror. With shock value.

Be wild. Be inventive. Bring in the Government, the Devil, the National Viewers and Listeners Society. Throw in Gamma Rays, Alpha Rays, vats of boiling acid, showers of sparks, lightning bolts, eerie mists floating off the moor, ancient curses, family curses, primitive taboos, the Illuminati, a full moon, a weirdly-glowing meteorite, a UFO, a native burial ground, and a family pet with an odd-coloured eye.

In short, make it up, and—

Make it juicy

Make it *good.*

Make it dramatic.

None of this "One day I was wandering in the woods and I found this old cabin and in the cabin there was this funny-looking bottle with 'Dangerous Monster Potion' on the label, and I thought, 'Ha! That can't really be a Dangerous Monster Potion, can it?' So I tried it, and suddenly I was a Dangerous Monster."

More like this: "I was struck by PURPLE LIGHTNING! THREE TIMES! Gah! Gah! Gah! And now I'm MAAAAAAAAAAAAAD!"

Do you see the difference between the two?

Imagine the effect at parties, job interviews and public hearings.

No one, but no one, can argue with purple lightning.

The Power of Exaggeration

"I was bitten by a spider."

Ho hum.

"I was bitten by a radioactive spider."

Mmm.

"I was bitten by a *giant* radioactive spider, with *two* heads."

Now we're getting somewhere.

You're a monster, right? And monsters ain't normal, right? So nothing *normal* is going to have made you into the monster that you are, right?

You want to think *big, big, BIG.*

There are two thresholds we must cross on the way to making an origin story. The first, as already mentioned, is the threshold between *truth* and *lies.* The second is from *lies* to *being so utterly over-the-top unbelievable you just have to believe it.*

I'll do you a diagram:

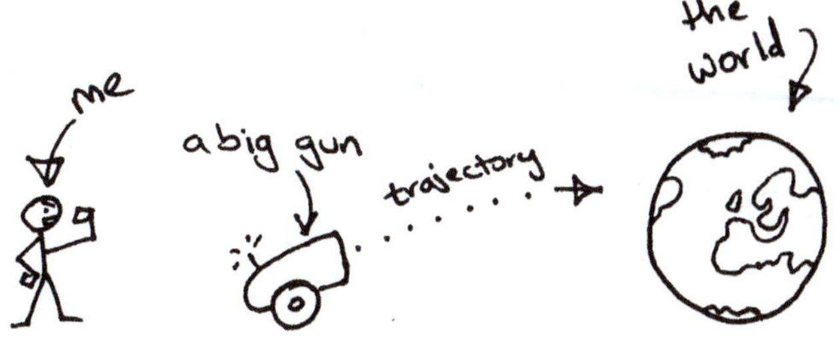

I didn't say it was a relevant diagram, did I?

Now, your origin story — get on with it.

Real-life stories: Bobby the Small-time Monster

Bobby was a small-time monster. His main monstrous aspect was a rather bad case of B.O. He used to walk around town muttering to himself, lingering rather too long in front of the women's fashion shops when they were dressing the mannequins. Eventually, Bobby crossed the line. Unable to contain his (frankly rather tepid) monstrousness any longer, he one day dashed into a shop, grabbed a mannequin, and ran off down the high street gibbering, "At last she's mine, she's mine."

Yeah, Bobby had problems. Most of all in terms of scale of ambition, but let's not hold that against him.

After all, the police didn't. No, what they held against him was theft of a shop mannequin and an unhealthy personal smell.

He went on trial. The prosecution put across a convincing case, complete with CCTV footage, the testimony of several sniggering shop assistants, and Bobby's mother, who said, "He always was a weird kid. He'd only watch the adverts on TV. He once tried to eat a fork. His dad was no better." His defence lawyer simply shrugged at the judge. The jury didn't even leave the room to come to their verdict. They gave the thumbs down sign in unison.

Finally, the judge turned to Bobby.

"And have you anything to say for yourself before I pass sentence?"

Bobby mumbled something.

"Speak up, man," the judge said.

Bobby said, "Vat of..."

"What's that?" the judge said.

Bobby said, "Strange... ray..."

The judge shook his head. "Enough of this nonsense. If you've nothing to say for yourself, remain quiet."

*And then, suddenly, as though the clouds had parted and a ray of Diabolical Inspiration had shone through, Bobby looked straight at the judge, eyes wide as golf balls and quivering like individual jellies, and said, "A space alien landed its UFO in the back garden when I was twelve. It gave me a potion to drink that was all bubbling and green. Then it operated on my brain. It inserted a live insect from the planet Zircolotta Minor that gave me the ability to read other people's thoughts. And suddenly I knew what everyone thought of me. How they hated me. And so I began to plot against them! To get my revenge! I was going to kidnap them, one by one, starting with the shop window mannequins! And I was going to build my own army, and implant live insects in **their** brains! Then the space alien will come back! It will come back and be impressed by what I've done! It will take me to its home planet, where I'll be proclaimed Emperor of the Universe! And they won't call me B.O. Bobby anymore! My personal odour will be made, by law, the most attractive odour in the Known Galaxy! I will be worshipped as a god! I will crush — you — puny hu-*

mans — with — my little — finger!"
They still locked him up.
I mean, the guy was clearly insane.

Conclusion

No possible origin story could ever account for just how
monstrous you really are. So, make something up. Don't
just blame your parents, blame the entire human race. Or,
blame a Mad Scientist. Nobody who's about to be devoured
by a monster wants to be told that the *reason* they're about
to be devoured by a monster is the monster's mother didn't
love him or her (or it) enough. The chances are, the victim's
mother didn't love *them* enough either. So, come up with
something dramatic and interesting. And, once you've come
up with it, forget the truth and believe the story. It's simpler,
easier, and, you're a monster, you ought to lie.

YOUR EVIL PLAN

Not all monsters need a plan. Your average Rampaging Monster tends to go with his or her gut (and their fangs, their claws, and that spike on the end of their tail that's so useful for batting cars, trains and people) on a moment-by-moment basis. But even Bob the Alien Blob, tired out after a hard day's, um, absorbing and enveloping, surely puts up its, er, pseudo-feet, lies back (or rolls back), and daydreams of World Domination.

That's a nice phrase, isn't it?

Say it aloud.

"World Domination."

(And if someone looks at you weirdly while you're saying it, try saying it again *looking straight into their eyes*. If that doesn't make them look away, they're weirder than you are.)

Now say it again, but say it oozing with desire. Really draw out the "o" in World and the "omination" in Domination. Because it's the *world* you want to dominate, and it's *domination* you want to do to the world.

I mean, isn't it?

What other plan *is* there?

Plans *other* than World Domination

Um, hello?

You *are* a monster, aren't you?

World Domination! World Domination! It's gotta be World Domination all the way, hasn't it?

Maybe not. There is, in fact, an alternative to World Domination.

World *Destruction*!

You want revenge? Of *course* you want revenge. But you don't just want to revenge yourself on those petty school bullies who made your adolescent life a misery. Come on, think big! Revenge yourself on the entire human race!

The only decision you've got to make about your Evil Plan is which of two extremely desirable end results you're after: World Domination or World Destruction.

Let's take a moment to do an exercise that should clarify which side of this delectable quandary you come down on.

Exercise: The world in your hand

I want you to get an egg.

Not an ostrich egg. Don't be flamboyant. Just a regular-sized hen's egg.

Sit it in the palm of your hand.

Now, this isn't an egg anymore. It's the world.

(If it helps, get out your paintbox and paint the oceans and the continents on your egg. Perhaps a few clouds, too. Maybe the sun glinting off the Pacific — wait, what are you DOING? You're a monster, not Leonardo Da Vinci! Paint the damn egg blue and green and get on with the exercise.)

Right, so the egg is the world.

Think of all the people on that world. Billions of them. Living in their little homes, with their little families, in their villages, their towns, their cities, their countries. Some of them have cute little hobbies like raising rabbits or collecting stamps. Some of them are in love. They send little text messages to each other saying "I luv U", with a cute picture of a cat. *See* them all, crowding this world in your hand, living their lives, dreaming their dreams, overcoming their daily struggles...

Got that?

Spend a moment, lingering on it.

Now...

(If you don't know what's coming next, you're really not monster material.)

CRUSH THE EGG!

Laugh as you crush it! Laugh monstrously! Laugh gleefully! Laugh maniacally!

Really crush that egg. Crush the little bits of it that are left. Then wash it all down the sink.

Doesn't that feel good?

Now for the telling point: which felt better, having the egg in your hand *knowing you could crush it at any moment*, or *actually crushing it*?

If *crushing it* felt better, you're a World Destruction type.

If you felt better before that, *knowing you could crush it any moment*, but not wanting to crush it because it felt too good knowing that you *could*, then you're a World Domination type.

Glad we've got that settled.

The details of your Evil Plan

Here's where you get to really express your individual monstrousness. Whether you want to Destroy the world or Dominate it, you've got to think how you're going to achieve this.

With Rampaging Monsters, it's easy. You're going to Rampage until (a) they give in to your demands and vote you World Ruler, or (b) you destroy everything.

Lurking Monsters have to be more creative.

Want to develop a Death Ray?

Want to create a race of Mechanical Killer Men who will terrorise the nations of the world?

Want to enslave humanity by sending hypnotic signals direct to their brains via their mobile phones?

Want to bring the Moon crashing down to the Earth in one almighty, death-dealing explosion — or at least threaten to?

Get creative. Come up with loads of ideas. Don't say no to any because they seem impractical — let's face it, they're *all* impractical. Given the fact that the world is, currently, neither destroyed nor dominated, the chances of a worm like *you* succeeding are frankly very small. Very, very small. So small that, were you in any way sensible or sane, you wouldn't even begin thinking about trying to attempt what you're right now thinking about trying to attempt.

But you're *not* sensible.

You're not *sane*.

You're a *monster*.

Your chances of success are beside the point. (Way beside the point. About twelve places right of the decimal, to be precise.)

Think of it this way: you are so absolutely bound to fail in any attempt you make to achieve your Evil Plan, that the best thing you can do is make your Evil Plan so monstrously, insanely over-the-top that it doesn't matter whether you succeed or fail — what matters is that you *thought* of it. That your monstrous, evil, deeply troubled brain latched onto such a monstrous, evil, deeply troubling plan — and took it seriously.

And so, as you lie there, dying from your final, fatal wound, you can shake your fist at your persecutors and say, "I was going to rule the world!" (Or destroy it.)

I mean, it's not quite the same if you're lying there dying from your final, fatal wound and you shake your fist and say, "I was going to invent a new flavour of sponge cake," is it?

Think big. Think really big.

Most of all, think insane, think monstrous, think evil.

The details of the plan don't matter.

Just *having* the plan — that's what counts.

Putting it in action

One more thing remains to be done.

Write up your Evil Plan, in as much juicy detail as possible.

Look at it every day.

Savour it.

Imagine it.

Feel it.

Because, frankly, that's as close as you're ever going to get to achieving it.

THE REVEAL

Some monsters are just naturally monstrous. You look at them, and can't help but think: "Ugh! What a hideous BEAST!"

Others have to work to achieve this effect.

Costume can be a key factor in determining people's (by which I mean, your victim's) reaction to you. A well-chosen get-up can make all the difference between their looking at you in polite disgust, or screaming their head off before fainting.

On the other hand, if you're one of those round-the-clock types who are always at their most monstrous, there are still techniques you can use to make your moments of actual monstrousness all the more effective. No one expects you to be sinking your fangs into your latest victim every moment of the day — such things have to be built up to, and even the most monstrous of monsters needs a little down-time afterwards (the Mummy had a few thousand years). So when it comes to the monstrous moment, you want to be at your best.

You want to make an impression.

And so, masked, cloaked, or *au naturel*, we now come to the subject I like to call the Reveal.

Masks

Are you a monster with a mask?

Masks are pretty useful for monsters. If you're basically hideous, but not *so* hideous that people are instantaneously powerless before the very sight of you — you might, say, simply have incredibly hairy nostrils, or a wart the size of a small hamster — a mask allows you to choose the moment when you reveal what hideousness you have *all in one go*, thus focusing the effect.

Choose your mask with care. There's no point going down to the local joke shop and buying a Frankenstein's Monster mask if you aren't at least three times as ugly, deformed, and downright shocking as old Frankenface himself. Otherwise, when you whip it off, people are just going to go, "Oh, that wasn't as bad as I was expecting."

NOT the reaction you're after.

A mask is all about *contrast*.

That's why the Phantom of the Opera — my vote for Monstrous Mask-wearer of the Millennium — went for a simple white half-face number, revealing just enough of the un-monstrous part of his phizog to lead his victim/special mate (see the chapter on Relationships for more on the special mate) into thinking he was just some normal-looking guy underneath.

And then off it comes! The moment of the Reveal! Ladies and Gentlemen, the horror in all its glory!

That's the effect you're after.

Cloaks

Think of it like this: a cloak is a mask for the *whole body*.

You want a cloak with a high collar, preferably with enough starch that it pokes up in two sharp points, because sharp points add to the general air of gothic monstrousness you're after.

A cloak should be long enough that it not only covers you entirely when raised, but has a little left over to billow eerily (silk is best at billowing eerily, nylon tends to billow more mundanely). You might want to practise giving little jerks of your arms underneath the cloak to initiate an eerie billow or two. (This might be necessary if there isn't a breeze.) Do it right, and it makes it look as though you inhabit your own supernatural weather system. (Do it wrong and it could look like you've just let rip and are trying to keep it under your cloak. Best to spend some time on this.)

A cloak should be black. Or red — dark red. Not pink, not Day-Glo yellow, or anything even remotely summery. Patterns — apart from very subtle dark-grey-on-black silhouettes of sinners writhing in Hell — are generally a bad idea. Flower-print doubly so. A cloak should allow you to hide in shadows, and suddenly open it to reveal your hideous, snarling, fang-filled maw. If you hide in flower-patches, you're going to have to have a *real* ugly mug to make a properly monstrous impression.

A final word on cloaks: get used to moving about in them *before* you venture out for a night's victim-hunting and terrorisation. There's nothing worse that spotting your intended prey, opening your cloak in the most dramatic way possible, and then, as you stalk towards your paralysed victim, tripping over its edge and falling flat on your face.

It ruins the effect.

Transformations

Masks and cloaks are all very well, but by far the best thing is if you're one of those fortunate monsters who physically change from normal human into full, monstrous mode when the need is upon them.

It may be a full moon, it may be the presence of eerily glowing Green Radiation (it's an actual scientific type), it may be that smoking potion you've just downed: whatever it is that sparks off your transformation, timing is crucial. If you know your favoured potion takes five minutes to achieve its effect, you're going to have to do some pretty serious planning if you want to transfix your victim by having them witness the spectacle of your horrific real-time monsterisation (as I like to call it). We all know how embarrassing it can be if you have to shuffle your feet, look at your watch, and say, "Just half a minute more. I can feel the tingling now."

If part of your transformation involves claws, spikes, bulging muscles, and various hairy lumps bursting through the seams of your day clothes, make sure you're wearing something flimsy enough that you can actually burst through. You don't want to get caught halfway, having to ask your would-be victim if they'll loosen your tie for you, because your hands are great useless claws now and the damned thing's choking you. And make sure you can rip the remaining rags off nice and sharpish — it will, shall we say, mollify the effect somewhat if you're chasing after your screaming prey with a Hello Kitty T-shirt hanging round your neck.

There's also the problem of being vulnerable while you are in the process of transformation. Most monstrous transformations incur a good deal of snarling, shuddering, writhing, drooling, growling and even screaming. And that's you, not your victim. You might have to pass a few vital seconds rolling on the ground while your toes turn to claws and push their way through your Crocs. (Seriously, though, a monster in Crocs? Or *anyone* in Crocs, for that matter...) If this gives your victim time to run away, you've already lost most of the advantage gained in transforming in front of them. If it gives them time to grab the nearest stout wooden pole, whittle it to a sharp point, harden it with fire, and drive it through your still-changing body, you seriously need to think about doing your transformation *beforehand.*

Snarls

Sometimes the old-fashioned ways are the best.

You're a monster, you've just cornered your victim and you want to, as it were, present your monstrous credentials, announce your devilish intentions — what are you going to do?

From the basest blubbering thing to the suave Count himself, nothing beats a good old-fashioned snarl. The ivory switchblade, as I like to call it.

It's the most basic of all reveals. You simply open your mouth. (Teeth clenched. No one's going to be scared if you just waggle your tongue at them, however green and warty it is.)

Surprisingly, this can still work if you're a non-fanged monster. *Any* sort of idiotic grin is scary in the right situation. Make a threatening noise, too — a hiss, a snarl, even something totally incomprehensible like "Gi-gi-gi-gloop!" and if you do it with enough conviction, it'll scare them.

Raise your clawed, or not-clawed, hands at the same time to add to the effect. Give your fingers a wiggle — though try not to make it seem you're about to tickle your victim. (Unless you do happen to be the Phantom Tickler of Old London Town. In which case, with chutzpah/idiocy like that, I assume you don't need my advice.)

One word of warning about snarls. They're all very well, but they can become a habit. If you snarl every time you corner your victim, they can get used to it and use it as an opportunity to run away. One snarl — one brief snarl, with optional lingering hiss if you plainly see your victim is terrified enough not to bolt — then go in with the fangs. Or the claws. Or the tickling stick.

"Gi-gi-gi-gloop!"

Terrifying.

Exercise: Practising your Reveal

It's no good arriving at the moment when your victim is quivering in terror as you loom over them, and you reach up to whip off your mask — only for it to get caught, and your grip slips, and the whole thing pings back on its elastic and slaps you in the face. Next thing you know, your contacts have fallen out and you're having to ask the very person you were about to maul to death if they'll help you scrabble about the pavement looking for them.

Or, you open up your cloak in one sudden, violent motion, and you get so tangled up in it you fall over.

Or, you bare your teeth for a good old snarl and bite your tongue in the process.

That's why you need to practise.

Now, I know what you're thinking. You're thinking, "Come on, I bet Count Dracula never spent hours working out how to sweep open his cape."

What are you talking about? Count Dracula is *hundreds of years old*. What do you think he does in his castle all night? He's spent more hours practising the sweep of his cape than you've spent *living*.

Conclusion

Every monster has his or her Reveal. With some it's a snarl that shows *just enough* fang. With others, it's dropping the mask. Or it may be a bit more complex. You might have to fall behind the nearest sofa, growling and howling, only to re-emerge transformed. As long as it doesn't involve you saying, "Hang on five minutes, let me get out of this truss," there's a good chance you can turn your Reveal into your most monstrous, frightening moment — the very essence of your monstrous YOU.

Make it something to be proud of.

(Or at least something that won't get you killed.)

YOUR FATAL WEAKNESS

Most monsters have a weakness. It may be an over-fondness for blancmange, a nervous habit like biting your (or someone else's) nails, or a total inability to be in the same room as an accordion player, but most likely it's going to be something more serious: a fatal aversion to fire, a tendency to frazzle in sunlight, a vulnerability to silver bullets (which, let's face it, is better than a vulnerability to *all* bullets, which is what the rest of us have), or a belief that climbing to the top of the tallest building in the city with your victim clutched in your enormous paw will save you from those pesky aeroplanes.

The question is, what to do about that fatal weakness of yours?

Write it down

Yes, write it down.

Preferably in some ancient language that only a few dusty academics can read, and preferably in some rare and fusty book that's kept locked up in an obscure, out-of-the-way library only accessible to dusty academics. Or, maybe, have it carved in an ancient runic script on your tomb so that only dusty academics can decipher it.

Then, start killing off dusty academics, one by one.

Spread a few myths

Or, yes, spread a few myths.

Folk tales.

Find a small number of ancient, wrinkled peasant-types, preferably the sort who have such thick, impenetrable accents that even their own families can no longer understand them — you know, the sort who make up peasanty-sounding words like "thilk" and "scroot" and throw in plenty of apostrophes when they speak — and have them learn a story or two about how your sort of monster can be defeated. Things that start with "On a full moon..." or "On the third Sunday of every second September..." or "When the chickariches croak in the bayou, and the wick-wolf howls..." Rubbish like that.

Then, start killing off ancient, wrinkled peasant-types one by one.

Or...

...maybe just shut up about it.

This is your weakness, yeah?

So don't tell anybody about it.

Unless you happen to belong to one of the more ancient, well-established types of monster like the werewolf or the old-fashioned vampire (as opposed to the new-fashioned vampire, who can do everything an old-fashioned vampire can't — gander about in the sun, wear a crucifix, sleep without a coffin, carry on a relationship with a non-vampire member of the opposite sex without draining them of all their blood — but have developed a new type of weakness that's almost indistinguishable from teenage moodiness), all of whose weaknesses are well-documented, and not just in folklore and mouldy old tomes in foreign languages, but in kid's books with bright colour pictures and 1-2-3 how-to-kill-a-monster instructions, the chances are nobody knows about your weakness but yourself.

So *keep quiet about it*.

Better yet, spread false rumours. Tell the world you're vulnerable to chocolate, or to being struck with a feather duster. Let it be known you can't stand the sight of your own (gorgeous) reflection. Have it said you're only vulnerable to mortal weapons when there's a "z" in the month (then stay away from foreign countries till you've checked the calendar).

I mean, if the monster-hunters are stupid enough to believe these silly lies, they frankly deserve what happens when they whap you in the face with that feather duster only to find you grinning back at them.

But just what is your weakness?

The chances are, though, that — unless you have a habit of poking yourself with a variety of implements to find out what hurts the most — you don't actually know what your fatal weakness is.

And you probably won't find out what it is — unless you're a dusty academic or like hanging around with them — until the actual moment when it's used against you. In other words, the moment when its fatality becomes fatally apparent.

By which time there's not much you can do about it.

Which leads nicely onto the subject of...

Your grisly death

Let's face it, with the exception of those of you who are already dead (zombies, I'm looking at you, and what an ugly lot you are), no one likes to think about their coming demise. But, being a monster, the chances are pretty high that at some point someone will come along and try to put an end to your Reign of Terror. And, judging by the evidence (or the movies on late-night TV, anyway), there's a good chance they'll succeed.

What can be done?

Picture the scene. You're cornered. Torch-wielding mob one way, heroic types with that vial of special fluid the other. You know the chances are against you. You're going to die.

Best thing to do?

Die with style!

And that means — you guessed it — practise.

Practise, practise, practise. I'm not going to say that being a monster is all about practise, because that would be lying. Being a monster is all about growling, howling, rending and raging. But a bit of practise helps. Particularly when it comes to your grisly death. Because, let's face it, you'll only get one stab at it (pun intended), so you might as well make a lasting impression.

Think about your grisly death. Your primary aim is to make it *grisly*.

(*They* supply the death, *you* supply the, um, gris.)

You'll want plenty of howling and screaming. Maybe some thrashing and writhing. You might foam at the mouth, preferably in an interesting colour. You might even want to dissolve in a heap of bubbling slime, if that's your style. The Mad Scientists among you might want to reserve enough time to get out a good Justification Speech, in which you sum up your life's aims, express your frustration at being thwarted so close to the moment of success, then end with a fading cry of "I will return!" as you fall off your parapet.

Think about it, plan it, practise it.

(Don't practise it to the extent of actually throwing yourself off a parapet, though. Let's not get carried away.)

And while you're doing that, why not think about...

Your grisly *fake* death

Because you don't *want* to die, do you?

(Or, zombies and vampires, you don't want to *un*-die, do you?)

You want to come back, for another Reign of Terror, another go at Ruling the World (or Destroying it), don't you? That's what being a monster is all about! A boundless desire to do evil, even from Beyond the Grave.

And the great news is, as a monster, you've got a good chance of coming back for a second, third, fourth or even fifth go. (I know this because I've seen it in the movies.)

Monsters have plenty of options. There's always a loop-hole. Those pesky monster-killers think they've killed you good and proper, but they missed a bit. Your little toe survived. And from that, some Mad Scientist can regenerate the Monstrous Whole of you. Or, some religious nut can regenerate you with a handy human blood sacrifice. Or you could come back as Son Of You. A slightly newer version, this time without the weakness that made you so easy to kill in the first place.

You might regenerate, reincarnate, or simply linger, like a bad smell, till the opportunity to reform and get back to your bad old ways comes along. You're used to lingering like a bad smell, aren't you? Most monsters are.

So why not simply fake your death in the first place? It does away with all the awkwardness of having to spend a decade or two slowly reconstituting your maimed and broken body from the odd rat or hobo who happens to pass by the spot of your grisly demise. Just be sure to always have a sachet of fake blood (or a packet of green goo, if that's more your style) ready whenever you're about to face your Arch Enemies.

Then, as soon as they come near, bite down on the sachet, froth you chosen colour of goo, writhe in agony (make it dramatic — it's only believable if it's so over-the-top un-believable that it comes all the way back round to being believable again), scream out curses, regrets, warnings, excerpts from your favourite poems, then burst into flames (that's optional) and rush from the room, announcing to all your imminent demise. Then fall off a cliff, leap from a rooftop, or simply sink into your coffin and close the lid. (All of these will have to be prepared for: a hidden hang-glider by the cliff; a rope for the rooftop leap; a bullet-proof, fire-proof, everything-proof coffin with the lock *on the inside.*)

Remember to give a fading, dying scream as you go.

Then, hole up in a (well-prepared) bolt-hole for a year or two, wait for the anniversary of your Terror to roll around again, and — *voilà*, you can venture out once more, terrifying cats and howling on the moors.

ALL MONSTERS ARE UNIQUE

As we have seen in the preceding chapters, there are many kinds of monster. There are Rampaging Monsters and there are Lurking Monsters. There are monsters who want to Destroy the World, and there are monsters who merely want to Dominate it. There are monsters with Evil Plans, and there are monsters who just like acting on impulse. (Or Rage, as we call it.) There are monsters in cloaks, monsters in masks, and probably even monsters in tutus, if you look hard enough.

When it comes down to it, there is only one thing all monsters have in common, and that is their uniqueness. Every monster is unique. Even the ones who are all the same, like zombies. Look at any crowd of zombies (not for too long — they may be shambling towards you at a very slow pace, but once they reach you, they'll eat your BRAIN), you'll see how individual each one is. This one has only half a head, that one is limping on a false leg. If you took the time, and really got to know them (I don't recommend it), you might find that one likes to bite his victims in the shin first, another likes to plunge his hands into their vitals and have a rummage for tasty bits. Each one is unique.

It's true of all monsters. What makes them unique makes them monstrous, and what makes them monstrous makes them unique.

Doesn't that produce a warm and fluffy feeling deep

inside?

Well, stop it now.

Revel in what makes you monstrous

In the chapter on Your Fatal Weakness, I said it's a good idea to know what your Fatal Weakness is, because that is the first step to avoiding it. But you shouldn't go through life (or un-life) fixating on your Fatal Weakness to the point that it's all you think about. Don't become like Vi the Vampire.

Real-life stories: Vi the Vampire

When Vi became a Vampire, the first thing she did was make a list of all the things she had to avoid. Crucifixes, daylight, holy water, running water, boring dinner parties. (That last one was on her list before she became a Vampire, but why drop it just because you're dead?)

*It was crucifixes that particularly bothered her. Did **any** cross count as a crucifix? Or any cross-shaped **thing**? She immediately removed the "x" key from her laptop, but what to do about the "Add as a Contact" button on her mobile phone? Did becoming undead mark the end of her social life? And what about the dozens of little kisses she used to get on the bottom of birthday cards? She didn't want to give up celebrating her birthday. One of the advantages of becoming a vampire, she thought, was that not only could she continue to celebrate her birthday, she could add her death-day as an excuse for a party, too. And what about the chance overlapping of tree branches — did **they** count as crosses?*

Pretty soon, Vi was too scared to leave her crypt.

She pined away, becoming more and more ghost-like every night.

She'd been so looking forward to becoming a vampire, to living a wild night-life, to digging her fangs into a wide variety of interesting throats, and now she was stuck indoors every night (and inside a coffin every day). It was all so disappointing. In fact it made her quite angry.

Then she realised that being angry meant being cross, and if she was cross, she must be a crucifix, and if she was a crucifix then there was no escaping it.

And so she frazzled away into a pile of dust.

Your strengths, not your weaknesses

What you should be thinking about is not your weaknesses, fatal or otherwise, but your strengths, your unique qualities, what *makes you* monstrous.

What, about your Monstrous Self, are *you* most proud of? What makes you feel most monstrous? What gives you that little kick of evil glee whenever you think of it?

Do you have a particularly insane-sounding plan for World Domination? Do you have a genuinely unique way of grinding your teeth when you're angry? Or a really good growl? A characteristic howl? A fine set of claws? Particularly hairy shoulders? Nice red eyes? Or perhaps you have a singularly offensive odour?

Whatever it is that makes you monstrous, *revel in it*. Bring it to the forefront of your monstrous identity. Start calling yourself The Red-Eyed Loon, if it's your red eyes you're particularly proud of. Or The Stinking Swampster, if it's your smell. If it's your wonderfully over-worked, mad-in-every-detail plan for World Domination, don't just have that plan scribbled out on a notepad you've chucked behind the sofa — type it up, choose a particularly eye-watering font, add some illustrations, print it out as a little brochure, and hand it to passersby wherever you go. Proclaim it from street corners, broadcast it on illegal bandwidths, post it on the internet. Call yourself Doktor Mad, the Mad Man with the Mad Plan and a BSc in Insanity, and have a lightning bolt tattooed to your forehead.

Don't do things by halves

Monsters don't do things by halves!

Monsters do things in-yer-face.

Monsters do things grotesquely, obscenely, atrociously, shockingly.

Monsters enjoy themselves, even when they're plummeting to their ultimate demise off the edge of a cliff. I mean, why not? If it's the last thing you'll ever do, you might as well get a kick out of it.

Monsters do things for the Hell of it. Quite literally. Monsters create their own special Hell, and then set about convincing/forcing the rest of the world to share in it.

Are you getting the idea, now?

Your Monstrous Life is all about revelling in your Monstrous Self.

No more excuses. No more shilly-shallying, no more dilly-dallying, or any other nonsense words for people who can't spell "procrastination". Time to stop procrastinating. Time to start crastinating. Or whatever.

Grrr.

YOUR MONSTROUS LIFE

Too embarrassed to admit his short-sightedness, Gogza pretended it had been Granny Ogden from the start.

RELATIONSHIPS

Generally, relationships between monsters and normal people are on a monster/victim basis. You are the monster, they are the victim. It's difficult to build a lasting, meaningful relationship this way, but you're a monster, what do you need with lasting, meaningful relationships? What do you need of normal people at all? I mean, other than the obvious (eating their brains, making them scream, turning them into one of you)?

Okay, there are a few cases. Let's have a look at them.

Your special victim

You may have a *special* victim. Often this is someone you knew before that terrible accident left you hideously scarred and bitterly resentful towards all normal people. Thinking of this special victim gives you vague, misty feelings of your one-time hopes and dreams, back when you weren't a monster.

So, obviously, the best thing to do is stalk, harass, scare and eventually kidnap that special victim, with the ultimate aim of forcing them to realise that, deep beneath your hideous exterior, you're still the same loveable person... Even though you *have* just stalked, harassed, scared, and kidnapped them, and are forcing them to relive those how-it-once-was feelings while strapped to a table with electrodes clipped to their most sensitive parts, and you standing before them unmasked and revealed in all your hideous, monstrous, unlovable glory.

I mean, it's a marriage made in Heaven, isn't it?

Your special mate

Monsters, being solitary creatures, rarely find a mate. Mostly, this is because they are unique (i.e., hideous mutants or the result of freak accidents), or because they are separated from their kin (by being frozen in ice for a million years, or by being stranded a billion light years from their home planet, for instance).

There are a few cases, though, where a monster *can* find a mate.

If you are undead — particularly if you are of, shall we say, the *long-term undead*, such as a thousand-year-old dried-out mummy, or an ancient vampire — and your one-time love has had the opportunity to reincarnate (or you can at least find someone who looks enough like them that you can convince yourself they're your long-lost loved one reincarnated), then maybe you've got a chance to build a lasting relationship. The initial problem, though, lies in convincing your reincarnated loved one to recall their previous life, and how they felt about you then, in the hope they'll somehow feel it again, and in sufficient quantity to overcome the fact that you're now a dried-out husk or a red-eyed ghoul and you live in a crypt. Usually this involves some sort of religious rite, preferably with a lot of woozy incense to make your chosen victim — sorry, *special mate* — lose most of their senses. Beware, though: your reincarnated mate may have developed other attachments in the thousands of years since you last met. Just a warning.

The other case where you stand a chance of acquiring a

special mate is if you happen to be either a mad scientist, or the creation of a mad scientist. If the former is true, all you have to do is brew up a special mate in your Vat of Bubbling Life (or, if robotics is your thing, make one out of old car parts); if the latter is true, apply to the mad scientist who created you and ask *them* to brew up a special mate in the same manner. (You may need to kidnap the mad scientist's own special mate in order to convince them. Try not to damage them too much in the process.) This one comes with a warning too, though. Life is unpredictable, and life created by a mad scientist even more so. You might well have a say in how your special mate looks, if you're brewing them up yourself, but you can never be sure how they'll react when they first see you. You are, after all, a hideous mess, a cast-off from humanity, a MONSTER. Your newly-created mate may be a monster, too, but they won't know that when they first wake up and see you. And first reactions are important. If they scream horribly and go insane at the sight of you, things might not go too well in the future.

Inter-species special mates

I know. It's weird. But you're a monster, you should be used to weird.

There you are, Primate Lord of the jungles of Skull Island, used to bossing it over dinosaurs and terrorising the natives, when you see her: the blonde. You've never seen a blonde before. It does something strange to your ape-ish insides. You feel, I don't know, less monstrous. Or *more* monstrous. All you know is that you *have* to whisk this blonde away in your fist, and keep her from harm. Even though she makes a funny, high-pitched screaming sound every time you lift her to your massive, simian face to get a closer look. You know the whole thing shouldn't work. She's five foot nothing, you're fifty foot and three inches.

She faints whenever you grin at her. But you just can't get that screaming blonde out of your head.

Or how about this. There you are, back end of evolutionary biology that you are, half fish, half man, living in your swamp, when along come a bunch of human scientists. One of them catches your eye. Who knows why? It's not like you could actually mate and produce children. You're half fish. Your reproductive method involves very little physical contact, and a lot of icky, gelatinous eggs laid thirty feet down at the bottom of a swamp. But there's something about this one. Maybe you just like their lack of scales. Or that high-pitched screaming sound they make whenever they see you. Sounds like the love-call of a dolphin, doesn't it? So you kidnap them, take them to your underwater cave, and gently drape them over a rock. It's going to be the start of beautiful relationship.

But here's the thing. In both cases: no, this is *not* going to be the start of a beautiful relationship. Apes and half-fishes don't mix well with humans, even blondes.

For a start, there's the disapproval of society to put up with. Usually, this takes the form of your chosen inter-species mate's companions coming after you with grenades, guns, dynamite, sleeping gas, nets, cages, and all sorts of other modern delights, so they can either kill you, or capture you and exhibit you in their home city. And your chosen inter-species mate might then come and visit you every so often (once they're free of your monstrous clutches, inter-species mates can develop a nostalgia for the utterly terrifying time you spent together, and may even feel quite fond of you — till you break free, grab them, and head for the nearest tall building, that is), but it's hardly the cosy future you were planning, is it?

I'm not going to be the one to tell you inter-species romances are difficult. I *will*, however, be the one to tell you they are dangerous, insane, and frankly icky. But you're a monster, you're not going to listen to advice, are you? The whole point of being a monster is to do insane things, act on your baser urges, and ignore advice.

So, if it floats your boat, I say give it a go.

It can only end tragically.

But, you're a monster. For you, *everything's* going to end tragically.

Torch-wielding mobs

Now we get to the other side of monster-human relationships.

This is where they start coming for *you*, rather than the other way round.

Such relationships can be tricky. I mean, usually they end with you trapped in a burning building or being driven off the edge of a cliff. I'd call such relationships tricky, wouldn't you?

It can be hard to form a relationship with a torch-wielding mob, mostly because — aside from the fact they want to kill you — they are, by definition, a mob, while you are but one. (Or, in the case of Bob the Alien Blob, a conglomerate of alien cells *acting* as one, but let's not get finickity, okay?)

You might want to try making the mob less a wall of mindless humanity by picking out individual faces. That angry old man there, didn't you throw his daughter down a well last week? And that sobbing woman, didn't you strangle her fiancé a mere fortnight ago? You see, you have a very personal relationship with these people. Not the sort that could ever lead to anything positive, I know, but it's something. And let's face it, in the world of monster-human relationships, we've got to take all we can get.

Those Pesky Kids, and other arch-enemies

Ah, yes, arch-enemies. Be it the gang of Pesky Kids (with optional dog) who ignore all parental advice to pry into the sort of dusty castles, ruined mansions and abandoned fairground rides you like to call home, or be it the ancient, foreign-sounding Monster Hunter who has spent a lifetime learning all there is to know about your type of monster (and somehow, even, managing to obtain academic qualifications because of it — why don't they give *you* the PhD? it's so unfair!), arch-enemies are like the torch-wielding mob who keep coming back.

And though this might sound like it's that much worse than a torch-wielding mob, you've got to look for the positives. "Keep coming back" means there's a chance for you to build a *real* relationship with that interfering gang of Pesky Kids, or that ancient, foreign-sounding Monster Hunter.

Think of it this way. If these people keep coming after you, there's obviously some grounds for common interest. They've got something *invested* in you. Frankly, they're probably secretly attracted to you. It's true, they may be showing all the signs of having worked very hard to assure your total and utter annihilation, and they may be making a very convincing attempt at not only killing you, but so utterly destroying you that there's no chance you'll ever reincarnate, regenerate, or return in any form whatsoever...

But the lengths they go to only show how much they *care*.

...Well, it's one way to look at it.

Even better, if you are regularly pursued by the same bunch of Pesky Kids, there's a real chance you might catch one's eye (not literally — best to leave their eyes intact, and it's probably the one with glasses you fancy anyway), and give them a knowing wink while their colleagues are busy trying to drive you backwards into your own Vat of Acid. After a while, such knowing winks can have their effect. They might give you a playful wink back. At which point you could say, "Why don't we ditch these losers and go and live in my castle?" And they might say, "I thought you'd never ask." And then you might—

What are you THINKING? This is *never going to happen*.

(Give yourself a good, hard slap in the face, right now.)

((And, can I have one, too?))

Those Pesky Kids might be cute, but they're no different from the hoary old Monster Hunter who's come out of retirement this umpteenth time to put you back in your grave. They just want to *kill* you. They just want the kudos of having slain you *again*. They just want to put your head up on their trophy wall.

Unless the hoary old Monster Hunter is the one you *really* fancy...

The point is, arch-enemies are the ones who keep coming back. In the lonely, twisted, emotionally empty world of the monster, this is the closest you're going to come to anything *like* a genuinely lasting relationship: someone who *so* wants to see you dead, they'll stick around for another go.

But, hey, let's not be conventional about this. If it works for them, and it works for you...

Henchmen

So, you have henchmen.

But seriously, relationships with henchmen?

Ick!

They're fodder. Fodder for the torch-wielding mobs and monster hunters. Don't get fond of them. Dress them up as you at the vital moment and use them as decoys while you escape.

Anything else than that is really just — yuck!

Loneliness

Because, let's face it, none of this really works does it?

People, I mean. Relationships with people.

You're a monster. Unique, monstrous, despicable, evil, horrendous, ugly. An outcast. An outsider.

By definition, a lone wolf.

(You may actually *be* a wolf. Some of the time, anyway.)

Okay, so there *are* monsters who go around in groups. Zombies, for instance. Zombies, and... Well, to be honest, I can only think of zombies. And, let's face it, once you're a zombie you're not likely to worry too much about relationships. You're only going to be worrying about eating people.

Anyway, this book isn't really aimed at zombies. Zombies don't read.

For the rest of us, then, a brief guide to a monster's only friend...

Loneliness.

(At this point, you might want to think about taking up the violin.)

But wait! No! Being a monster is not about feeling sorry for yourself. (Except in violent, revenge-filled rages about how society has ignored, reviled and scorned you. *Then* you can feel sorry for yourself. But only spectacularly.)

For the rest of the time, don't think of it so much as loneliness. Think of it as having your own way *all the time*. Think of it as a rehearsal for that moment when you've finally wiped every other living thing off the face of the planet and can finally get some peace and quiet. Think of it as your natural state.

In other words, *get used to it*.

You're a monster. Chances are, you're going to spend an awful lot of time on your own in a dank, dark cave.

Try taking up a hobby. Something for those between-victims moments. Crochet, perhaps, or Sudoku. Or you might raise pets. Piranha. Sharks. Crocodiles. Flesh-eating ants. Killer bees. That sort of thing. Give them names. Let them have a nip of your finger every so often.

It's the closest thing you're going to get to a real relationship, you foul scum of existence, and you know it.

Take-away points

How to sum up this brief but nevertheless profoundly disturbing look at human-monster relationships?

You are a monster. They are normal human beings. There's no way it's going to work.

Not in anything approaching a manner that could be described as normal way, anyway.

So, the best thing to do is find a way of taking what you can out of whatever twisted, perverted, morbid relationships you *do* form. It's that or nothing.

And if you think that's depressing, the next chapter's about work.

WORK

Wouldn't it be lovely if you could simply *be* a monster *all* the time? If you didn't have to worry about bills, the mortgage, where the next meal was coming from? If people at parties accepted you for who you are, rather than saying, "And what do you do?" with a look that implies, whatever the answer is, it's not going to be good enough.

Work, like death, disease, taxation and war, is an integral part of the way our society operates, and as such has to be tolerated, or at least struggled through with gritted teeth.

But this doesn't mean the hours of 9a.m. to 5:30p.m should make up your daily dose of unremitting, living Hell. After all, there's shift work and overtime to consider, too.

So, until you really do destroy/dominate the world, let's look at various monstrous strategies for getting through the un-monstrous part of your day.

Choosing a career

The only genuine career you'll ever have is your own Career of Monstrousness. Your Career of Evil. Everything else is just stuff you have to do to get by.

Or is it? You might be lucky enough to have the aptitude for a career that accepts monstrousness as normal — that encourages, even nurtures it.

Banking, for instance, or politics.

The only trouble with this approach is that you may find your monstrous energies being sapped by the work you do for others. Evil Scientists who spend all day designing weapons for someone else may find they lack the energy to come home and spend all night designing yet *more* killer robots and mega-destructive doodads for their own wicked purposes.

(This may, in the end, make no difference to you. Your weapons or somebody else's weapons, what does it matter so long as they make a loud bang and kill people? Just so long as they're not pointed at you, yes?)

Most probably, your monstrous skill-set may not be especially fitted to a particular career. There isn't much call for the ability to turn into a bat at will, or for having a proven track record in stomping on freight trains. However, your generally monstrous demeanour can still land you a job. Many firms have opportunities available for psychopaths and borderline head-cases, usually in lower management. The whole point of such whip-cracking roles is to keep the lowest-paid employees (who actually do the work) from discovering that there is a tier of the company above them who are paid a lot more to do a lot less. Often with bonuses. Such gatekeeper positions are perfect for people with an off-putting personality, poor manners, bad hygiene, shouty inter-personal skills, and an inability to make genuine friends. Perfect, in other words, for us monsters.

Still another mode of career you can adopt is to find some work where you can exist largely unseen, thus keeping your inner monstrousness hidden during daylight hours. You may be a monstrous slavering wolf-creature at night, but you can be a mouse at work, doing your job as expected, barely scraping by with your targets met, never receiving a promotion or a demotion, never speaking up at meetings, always doing your turn at getting the coffees. Then at night you howl like a mad thing. Plus, the knowledge that you could, at any moment, throw off your mousey shackles and rampage in monstrous form throughout the office, trashing computers, photocopiers, ergonomically designed chairs and the odd water cooler, can help to get you through the daily frustrations created by such keep-it-all-bottled-inside career paths.

Promotion

However monstrous we are, we are also, to some extent, lamentably human. This means we have human needs as well as monstrous needs. I'm not talking about anything icky here. I'm talking about the need to prove yourself as someone above the common herd — as, in fact, a leader, not a follower.

I'm talking about promotion.

There are many legitimate strategies for getting promotion. They might include working very hard, staying late hours, "going the extra mile", or even simply walking into the boss's office and throwing a mega-tantrum. These strategies are all written about in other books

We are here to talk about monstrous strategies.

Here are some ideas:

- Rather than working extra hard yourself, find a weaker-willed member of staff and bully them into doing the additional work for you. That way, not only do you get to tell your boss how much more work you've been doing recently, but you can compare yourself favourably to that member of staff whose production has been getting distinctly lax of late (because they've been doing so much work for you).

- While being interviewed for the new position, let out the occasional growl or bark, and perhaps a hungry grin. This has the dual effect of (a) letting your interviewer know how much you want the position while (b) subtly threatening them with the possibility that you might eat them if they don't give it to you. Plus, an ability to growl, bark, and grin evilly might be the very qualities they're looking for.
- Eliminate all competition. I'm not going to go into details, because we're all monsters here, right?

Finding fulfilment at work

You are a monster.

You find fulfilment through being monstrous.

You be monstrous through expressing those individual aspects of yourself that are so wonderfully monstrous.

Work does its best to quash all that. The perfect work-slave is a nine-to-fiver with no more ambition than the security of a regular payslip and the promise of a week off in summer, and no more individuality than an amoeba.

Monstrousness and work are a pair of opposites that are never going to be reconciled.

Am I being a tad negative?

Well, if I am, what do you expect from a frustrated world-destroyer currently locked in a padded cell with only a crayon between my toes for company?

Okay, maybe work *can* have its benefits. You get paid. You... You get paid. Um...

Look, at school, I'm the one who attacked the careers advisor with a stapler, okay? Don't expect advice from me. Certainly not any advice on finding fulfilment at work. You get through the day, that's what you do, fuelled by fantasies of revenge, plans for world domination, and the occasional chat with Nancy from Accounts, who you suspect may be a monster just like you.

The rest of the time is Hell. Sheer, unrelenting, dreary, soul-destroying, emotion-deadening, sanity-wrenching Hell.

But you're a monster. Your *life* is Hell. You're used to it.

And that is about the best thing I can say on the subject.

Let's finish with a real-life story. Not because it's relevant, but because I need cheering up.

Real-life story: Frank the Stain

Frank was an unusual type of monster. He wasn't a hairy beast with fangs, he wasn't a screaming lizard with claws. He was a stain. A walking stain. Hard to imagine, I know, but that's what he was.

Frank had difficulty getting a job. In fact, because he was a walking stain, he couldn't fill in job application forms, write a c.v., use the telephone or conduct himself with any sort of dignity at interviews. All he could do was be a stain.

Things seemed pretty tough for ol' Frank.

He wandered the streets of his home town, kicking up dust, forlorn.

Pretty depressing, eh?

Well, actually this story doesn't have an ending, so it'll have to stay depressing.

Gee, I was hoping to cheer myself up.

Let's try another one.

Real-life story: Wendy the Witchmonster

Wendy was a Witchmonster. Not a witch, but a witchmonster.

What's the difference, you ask?

Well, a witch can brew up potions, fly on a broomstick, cackle madly, turn herself into a variety of domestic animals, and put curses on people. A witchmonster is just an ugly monster. She can cackle madly, but that's about it. Generally, witchmonsters are a lot less good at anything impressive than witches. Except they have a better name.

Now we've got that settled, on with the story:

Wendy had difficulty getting a job. (Oh dear. I've a feeling this might be as depressing as the last real-life story.) Unlike Frank, though, she could fill in job application forms, write a c.v., use the telephone and conduct herself with a modicum of dignity at interviews. But she tended not to, as the only thing she really liked in life was cackling madly.

She was good at cackling madly. She could really hit those scratchy, nails-on-slate notes that make your hair stand on end. She could do an utterly chilling belly laugh and make it rise seamlessly to a banshee-scream that would turn you to ice. This was the one thing she was good at.

She put it on her c.v., in big letters. (She used big letters because she didn't have anything else to put on her c.v.)

Unfortunately, cackling madly isn't a quality employers look for in a potential worker.

Wendy didn't get any jobs.

So, she decided to take things into her own hands. She stood on street corners and cackled for free. She'd frighten children, old people, passersby, residents — anyone and everyone who happened to be around. Eventually, she was locked up in a nice warm cell, where she was fed regular meals, and even allowed to watch TV — at which she would cackle madly.

So, hey, she never got a job, but she didn't need to, did she?

(Whew! I thought that one was going to end as badly as the Frank the Stain one. Who says there aren't any happy endings in the world of monsters?)

LIVING WITH THE CONSEQUENCES

Guilt. Shame. Regret.

That's my average weekend.

But also, luckily enough, it's the subject of our current chapter.

What we're talking about here is the aftermath of your monstrous deeds. The moment when you confront that icky, gunky mess left over from your latest escapade, and see it for what it really is: nothing but eyeballs and bits of goo. The moment when the monstrous glee that drove you into your riot of growling, howling, yowling and fouling (we all do it) departs and you're left deflated, despondent, in desperate need of a shower and even, yes, questioning your wish to be a monster.

Did you do the right thing donning that mask, that cloak, quaffing that potion?

No.

You didn't.

But — you're a *monster*.

You *never* do the *right thing*.

You always do the *wrong thing*. That's what being a monster's all about.

It means the guilt, the shame and the regret are all going to be a normal part of your everyday life from now on, hanging around you constantly like those nasty bodily smells you've been trying to disown all these years. In other words, better get used to them.

Depressing, huh?

Well, it doesn't have to be.

I am, after all, the man who laughs in the face of guilt, chuckles at the hackles of shame, and guffaws into the gut of regret. (I actually giggle helplessly at everything, from exploding kittens to tax bills. That's why they locked me up.)

Fortunately, I am sufficiently in command of what I laughingly refer to as "my senses" to know that there are several approaches you can take in facing the three-headed dog that comes snuffling around whenever you take the time to reflect on the monstrous things you've done. Because that's all it is: guilt, shame, regret — just a great big hairy mutt, with bad breath, slobbering jowls, and a tendency to lick its own private parts in awkward social situations.

Time to teach this old dog some new tricks.

What every zombie knows

Do you think zombies feel guilt?

Do you think zombies feel shame?

Do you think zombies feel regret?

Actually, I'm pretty sure zombies don't feel anything. Except perhaps a constant, aching hunger for the soft inner parts of the living.

They are, after all, dead. They just happen to be walking around. (The same might well be said of a lot of so-called Normal People.)

Isn't there something we can learn, then, from these fine, shambling folk? (The zombies, not the Normal People.)

How about: Nothing seems quite so bad once you're no longer alive?

Hmm.

Not great, as advice goes, but it's *something*. And let's face it, monsters, we need all the help we can get.

That painting in your attic

Wouldn't it be great if you could take all that guilt, all that shame, all that regret, and put it somewhere else? Not have to feel it at all? Just put it away, like money in a bank, then forget about it?

Of course, the trouble with money in a bank is it tends to accrue interest. This is good in the case of money, but bad in the case of guilt, shame, and regret. In fact, comparing guilt, shame and regret to money in a bank was a bad idea from the start.

Let's try again...

Wouldn't it be great if you could take all that guilt, all that shame, all that regret and put it away somewhere else? Like water in a great big reservoir, held back by a dam. And slowly, as the water rises, and the dam starts to crack with the pressure...

That's no good either.

Try again...

Wouldn't it be great if you could take all that guilt, all that shame, all that regret and put it away somewhere else? Just hide it away, like disposing of an awkward piece of evidence — a victim's car, perhaps — in that handy swamp just outside town? I mean, once it's sunk out of sight, what's the chance of it bobbing back up again? Till the swamp gets full, that is, or a great bubble of marsh gas brings the car back up...

Oh, this isn't any good either.

One more time:

Wouldn't it be great (blah blah blah) if you could take all that guilt, all that shame, all that regret (blah blah blah) and put it away somewhere else? Just put it away, like, um... a painting in your attic?

Now, stick with me on this one.

Then you could have the painting in your attic — somehow, magically — take on the burden of all your bad deeds. That way, whenever you did something bad, the *painting* would look worse, but *you* would stay the same. And slowly, all those terrible deeds that ought to have made your once-devilishly-handsome face look simply demonic would accumulate on the face in the painting, while your own face would continue to look as fresh, as young, and as devilishly handsome as ever.

I mean... what a stupid idea, yeah? The only way this is going to work is if you actually go up into the attic yourself and, every time you do something a little naughty, paint on a wrinkle or a scar or a wart or something. And at the end of it you'll have this damned ugly portrait that once looked like you, but you yourself will *still* have got older, and all that guilt, shame and regret will *still* have done its work on you.

Let's face it, it's a *dumb idea*.

They're *all* dumb ideas.

Hide anything away and it just comes back — often, worse than before. There's no amount of Self-Helpery, jiggery-pokery, affirmation arm-waving, visualisation nonsense that's going to make you forget all the horrible things you've done and how bad they really make you feel. About the only thing that'll do that is a frontal lobotomy, and those, let me tell you, are not cheap.

There's only one idea that's going to work, here, and that's:

Pigs in mud

Pigs in mud.

Yep, that's my idea.

Listen:

Does a pig like mud?

You bet it does.

It wallows in it. It rolls in it. It doesn't even care if it's mud, or something worse. (You know what I'm talking about.)

A pig lives in mud, and the pig likes it.

A monster lives in bad deeds, and the "mud" of bad deeds is guilt, shame, and regret. A monster should learn to wallow in mud. If you happen to be a were-pig, this is just going to be *so* easy. But it doesn't have to be actual, literal mud. It can be other sorts of icky substances. Count Dracula (my hero) may be suave and sophisticated, but he can be bathed in blood from his fangs to his cummerbund and he doesn't care. He *likes* it. Think he spends a moment on guilt, shame, or regret? Not one bit. He slurps up the red stuff, then turns into a bat and flaps off into the night, happy as Larry. (Unless Larry happened to be his last victim. In which case, he's far, far happier than Larry.)

The way to deal with monstrous guilt, shame, and regret is not to let them weigh on you. What you have to do is learn to take a whole new joy in them. In fact, you should learn to respond to guilt, shame and regret with Monstrous Glee. (Remember Monstrous Glee? Just because it was in an early chapter doesn't mean you're being let off practising it.) The guilt, shame, and regret that hit you once you've done something really monstrous are actually like the little gold stars your teacher never gave you in school because you were always picking your nose in class. They're like an inner confirmation of your slimy-souled monstrousness. They are your new good. They are your new happiness. They are the air you breathe and the food you eat. They are *you*.

To aid you in making the necessary mental shift towards this new outlook on guilt, shame and regret, how about a little exercise?

Exercise: "Only that I didn't do more..."

So you've done your monstrous deed, and for a moment you felt really good about it. Really *evilly* good. Then, the inevitable downturn. The sigh, the slump, the leaden weight in your gut. The nagging guilt, the pummelling shame, the oodles of regret.

Time to turn that around.

Let's say, then, that you feel the start of a little guilt tugging at your conscience.

Don't pretend it's not there. Don't try to hide it, or bury it, or ignore it.

Turn and *face* it.

Say: "Do I feel guilty?"

And answer that question with: "Only that I didn't do *more*!"

Now, let's say a bit of shame starts to creep into your otherwise dark, sticky, and poisonous heart.

Turn and *face* it.

Say to it: "Do I feel ashamed?"

And immediately answer: "Only that I wasn't even *more* despicable!"

Then, let's say you start to feel regret sinking into your gut like a lead pill.

Turn and *face* it.

"Do I feel regret?"

"Only that I can't be doing it *again*, now, *twice* as much!"

Then indulge in as much Monstrous Glee as you can manage.

Your one true special victim

Now it's time to reveal one of the Deep Secrets of Monstrousness.

Let me introduce you to your one, true, special victim.

No, it's not that blonde who lured you out of the jungle to the bright lights of the city, only to trap you in a cage and leave you for a Normal Human. And no, it's not that sweet young thing who loved you once, before your hideous accident, and who has since taken up with a far more handsome/beautiful, rich do-gooder who actually remembers things like birthdays and anniversaries.

It's none of those.

It's you.

Yes, you.

To be specific, it's your conscience.

Your sense of right and wrong.

Your sense of social propriety.

It's that nagging inner parent that says you shouldn't have done what you've just done.

What you have to do is *murder* it.

Kill it stone dead.

Oh, it'll come back, night after night, nagging, whining, screaming and crying. "What have you made of yourself?" it'll say.

So murder it again.

Don't see it as the innocent, playful child you once were, confronting the monstrous, guilt-encrusted devil you now are. It's not that. The innocent, playful child you once were was actually a total monster, too, only you don't remember it like that. The innocent, playful child picked its nose, broke things, squashed insects for fun, and was generally far more evil than you are now, even after all these years of practice. It was taught to fit in, you see, to be like other people (or at least to feel bad for not being like them), to toe the line, to act the part, to wear the mask of a Normal Person.

So don't feel too bad. Murder your conscience, the part of you that says "No", and "Just look at what you're doing!" Murder it. Feel free for a moment...

Then, when the guilt, the shame, and the regret for *that* hits you—

You can come and join me in the asylum, my dears!

You'll *like* it in the asylum!

We sing and play all day, here!

They give us crayons!

And we laugh! We laugh! We laugh so much our jaws ache with laughing but still we have to keep on laughing — because we can't stop!

We're all monsters here...

In the asylum...

NOW YOU'RE ON YOUR OWN

**_"If at first you don't succeed... trash
the place."_**

So that's it. I have no more wisdom to impart (not that any of it was wisdom, anyway, just stuff I made up), no more lessons to teach, and my crayon is now at that difficult, stubby stage, too short to wield with any accuracy between my toes, but too long for the warden to consider giving me another one.

From here on, you're on your own.

Disappointed?

Perhaps you expected, at this stage, to be fully transformed into a giant, fire-breathing mega-lizard, rampaging around your local metropolis, chomping on passenger vehicles of all sizes?

That was never going to happen.

Perhaps, then, you expected at least to have grown a few more hairy patches, to have slightly sharper teeth, and slightly more claw-like hands, or perhaps you wanted to have developed a cobra-like hypnotic stare, or the ability to turn yourself, at will, into a wolf or a bat or some other creature of the night?

Well, that was never going to happen either.

Frankly, I think you should count yourself lucky if you came away from reading this book with a slightly deeper growl, a slightly stronger scowl, and maybe a small scar or two.

Being a monster isn't easy. Becoming one is even less so. Just think of the caterpillar in its chrysalis. It has to turn itself into goo before it can become a butterfly. And let me tell you, turning yourself into goo isn't easy. (I've tried it. It was messy.)

Being a Normal Human isn't easy either, but, balancing one against the other, point for point, I think being a monster is easier than being a Normal Human. As a monster, you have at least resolved those awkward inner conflicts, those should-I-or-shouldn't-I moments (the answer is always "Yes, I should, and as nastily as possible") once and for all. And you may still suffer guilt, shame and regret, but at least you *expect* to, and have moved that little bit further on the road to *enjoying* them.

Plus, you always have your Monstrous Glee to fall back on.

What do Normal Humans have? Love, friendship, camaraderie, the quiet knowledge they've got savings in the bank, a family at home, a job that earns them a modicum of respect... Yuck! I say, yuck! Give me my tatty-walled cell any day. Give me my crayon, my evil dreams, and my as-yet-unfinished Master Plan for Destroying the World. Give me my Evil Laugh, my Insane Chuckle, and my Delirious Cackle. Give me my moments of Rage. Give me my Reasons for Wanting Revenge. Give me my Resentments, my Guilts, my Shames, my Regrets.

I mean, without them, what have I got?

A rather shabby cell, and crayon crumbs between my toes.

I've enjoyed this time we've spent together. Me in my cell, you in your — wherever. (I like to picture you in a dank, dark cave, with a constant, clock-like dripping sound all around you, and perhaps slime on the walls. Most likely, you're reading this on the train, flashing the occasional furtive glance at your fellow passengers, wondering if they're reading the same book, and worried they might be getting ready to unleash *their* plan for World Destruction before you've even thought of yours.)

We've had good times, yes?

Remember the chapter on Your Evil Plan?

Ah, yes...

And the one about Your Fatal Weakness?

Ah, yes, yes, yes...

And the one about Brewing an Invincibility Potion?

Oh, I left that one out.

Ah, well. Maybe in the second edition.

If they let me have another crayon.

If they let me have more paper.

If they let me have my royalties.

Or perhaps, I could tell *you* in person? Whisper it, through the wall. I mean, you *are* coming to join me, aren't you? That was the only reason I wrote this book, really. It gets so lonely in here. Even when the halls resound with the sound of manic laughter, there's a feeling that I don't really get on with my fellow inmates. I thought maybe if you, unbalanced by reading this frankly insane book, finally cracked and got put away here, in the empty cell next to me, perhaps we could become friends? Share our plans for World Domination. And perhaps you could ask the warden for a crayon, and give it to me, so I can write another book, and get us more friends?

What do you say?

No?

Oh well, you can go to Hell, then.

ABOUT THE AUTHOR

Murray Ewing was born in 1971 in Reading, England. Among the usual variety of strange jobs writers are supposed to have, he's worked as a vitamin packer, porter at a mushroom farm, postman, and computer programmer.

For more, visit his website:

www.murrayewing.co.uk

I think you'll agree, the less known about Edweard Deadwitt, the better…